KILLER EDGE

CHET CUNNINGHAM

Killer Edge
Paperback Edition
Copyright © 2025 (As Revised) Chet Cunningham

Dark Wolf Books
An Imprint of Wolfpack Publishing
701 S. Howard Ave. 106-324
Tampa, FL 33609

www.darkwolfbooks.com

Paperback ISBN 979-8-89567-906-7
eBook ISBN 979-8-89567-905-0

KILLER EDGE

1

Forest Glen, Oregon. September 24th

WILLY HASKINS KICKED a stone at the side of School Lane, the street that led into town from Forest Glen High. What a bummer. He had called three guys to come give him a lift home after practice and they all bombed out on him. Some kind of best friends. One was grounded after school. Another one had lost his driver's license. The third one was at a girl's house. Double bummer. So he had to walk the mile and a half. All because that judge had yanked his driver's license for three months for reckless driving. They were just having a little fun. Anyway, Joey liked to ride on the car's hood as they streaked past the Tip Top with the horn blasting and Joey screaming like an idiot. Of course Joey was brain dead and crazy as a fullback. Willy hated to walk. He had no choice now. He zipped up his letterman's jacket with the big FG on it and the two football symbols. Maybe the jacket would help him get a ride. Not many cars on this road.

Five minutes later, Willy heard a car coming up behind him. He half turned and held out his thumb. Some old jalopy, but what the hell, he was desperate. Practice had been grueling today and he was worn down to a nub. To his surprise the car slowed and then stopped just past him. Willy walked up to the passenger's side window and looked in.

"Need a ride?" some older dude asked. Willy had never seen him before. He had to be almost thirty.

"Yeah, my feet are killing me."

"Jump in. Where you going?"

Willy opened the door, thankful that it didn't fall off in his hands, and stepped in. The inside of the rig was a mess. Reminded him of his own bucket of bolts. The seat belt had been cut off.

"Where am I going? Just into town near the Tip Top."

"Get you there in a shake." The driver suppressed a grin. This was going to be easier than he figured. A three-pointer his first time out looking for this particular high school boy.

The kid glanced up at the driver. "Man I sure could use an ice cold Coke about now."

"We're on our way. Hey aren't you Willy Haskins, the Tiger's quarterback? I go to all the games. That was a great touchdown pass Friday night."

Willy grinned. "Yeah that was awesome. Best in the West I say. Another good game and I should get a lot of notice by the college scouts."

The driver nodded. "Yeah you might make it. Hey, you want a beer? I keep some cold ones in back."

"Against the law to have an opened container....."

Willy broke it off and they both laughed. "Why not? Sure a beer."

The driver smiled, "Good. I need one, too. Let me get off this street and drive down a ways where the cops won't spot us. Okay?"

"Oh yeah. For a cold beer, okay."

THE NEXT MORNING just after six a.m. Officer Hardy Jones clawed his way out of bed and reached for the phone. He got it on the third ring. What was it this time? Had to be cop business. He was in no mood to be rousted out of bed again in the middle....

"Yeah, Jones here."

"We have a problem, Hardy." It was Police Chief Sanderson. "Got a dead body out on String Town Road about a mile off the highway. Some biker found it and called in. I'm on my way. I'll see you there."

"Right Chief. I'm grabbing my pants." Hardy Jones's wife, Cindy, leaned up on one elbow and rubbed her eyes. She hated these late night and early morning calls. She brushed back long blonde hair and frowned. "You got to go in?"

"Yeah, dead body out on String Town Road. Be home when I can make it." Hardy let out a sigh as he dressed. Sometimes he hated it here where their whole police force was four officers and the chief. City council kept trying to cut one man. The mayor had said, "How many cops do you need to handle a huge town like Forest Glen of three thousand people?" Hardy could have gone to Portland, got into a real police department, maybe moved up. But, no, he had to stay in his home town and be a small potatoes cop. One traffic light hick town. The problem was he loved this little berg and he had been born here.

Hardy Jones was two inches under six feet, sturdy, strong upper body, and had weightlifter's arms. His face was cut from old leather, with a solid chin, small nose, and darting always moving green eyes. He kept his dark hair barbered to the proper law enforcement length.

Twenty minutes later Officer Jones wheeled his blue two year old Ford to the side of the road behind Chief Sanderson's city cruiser and hurried up to five people in a field just off String Town Road. Jones shook his head as he read the scene. A boy, maybe sixteen to nineteen, naked, on his back, and with deep purple ligature marks on the front of his throat.

"Chief, I checked on the way out. Most of this road is in the city limits. It extends out to the sewage treatment plant. So it's our jurisdiction."

Chief Sanderson scowled. He was fifty next month, twenty pounds overweight, thinning black hair with touches of gray, and a perpetual grimace designed to keep people at a distance. It worked. He had been a cop in Portland for twenty years and came out to this small town to slow down a little. For sport he was a bow and arrow hunter. Bagged his first two-point buck last fall. "I called the county sheriff's office. They're sending out two detectives and their two man forensics team. Let's get back away from the scene so we don't mess up any clues that might be here. Looks clean to me so we won't have squat to go on."

Jones saw day shift officer Al Turley talking to a man in his twenties holding a bike. Turley would get what the finder knew and put in his report.

Officer Jones took another look at the victim's face. It was unmarked. "Oh, wow, Chief. I know the kid. He's Willy Haskins. The high school football quarterback. His picture was in the paper last week."

"Oh yeah. I've seen him play. He was good. Not much else to watch around here but high school sports. Half the town was there Friday night. Kid threw a great touchdown pass." The Chief answered his cell phone and put it away. "The county will send out an assistant Medical Examiner. So we wait for him."

The Chief, Jones, the two day shift cops, and the biker moved back twenty yards from the body. The two day officers went back to their assigned duties. The biker talked with the chief a minute then rode off. Jones brought his brows down to half hood his eyes. It was a bad habit and telegraphed that he was deep in thought.

"Chief, you remember who the kid's dad is?"

"Yeah. He runs the hardware store, Lawson Haskins."

"Think we should call him to come take a look and see if we can get a positive I.D.?"

Chief Sanderson kicked at the weeds and swore softly. "This is the part of the job that I hate. You're sure that the boy is Willy Haskins?"

"On a stack of Bibles. He was street drag racing and reckless driving a month ago. I caught him and his license was suspended."

Chief Sanderson nodded and took out his cell phone. Two cars growled up to the side of the road and the county troops bailed out. Two detectives in suits, the sheriff himself in uniform, and an assistant ME with his little black bag.

The two man forensic team came out of the second

car with stakes, crime scene tape, and their bag of tools. They staked out a twenty yard circle around the body and went to work. The ME knelt beside the body, turned it over, and then back.

"Only signs of violence are two minor contusions on his head and the ligature marks on his throat," the ME said. "Preliminary has to be strangulation. I'll give you something definite after the autopsy tomorrow."

"What about the time of death?" Hardy asked.

The ME hesitated. "Not sure. Give you a range figure. From the rigor mortis setting in, I'd say the death came about two to three a.m. Could go two hours earlier."

Chief Sanderson and the Sheriff talked. The sheriff had been a field cop for twenty years and couldn't keep away from the big cases. He carried an Ingram subma-chine gun in a locked box in his car.

"No slimy perp is gonna outgun me," he told anyone who asked about the sub gun.

"Chief, it's your party. Anything we can do to help is yours. If it is just strangulation, that makes it tougher. No murder weapon."

"I don't remember when we had the last murder here in town," Chief Sanderson said. "Must be at least ten years. We'll take all the help your forensic guys can find."

Hardy Jones shuffled through the foot high weeds and grass just outside the forensic men's yellow crime scene tape. Who would want to kill the Tiger's star quarterback? Who? It didn't make sense. Was it connected to the football team at the school? Or was it a random target of opportunity? Hardy watched the forensics guys. They were yelling at each other and showing signs of frustration that usually meant that they were finding zilch in the way of clues. The ME had closed up his case and left a half hour ago. The forensics guys kept looking.

A white Honda raced up String Town Road toward the crime scene. It skidded to a stop half on and half off the road. The driver's door jolted open, a man in his forties jumped out of the car, and stormed toward the yellow tape. Before anyone could stop him, the man charged through the tape breaking it in three places and raced up to the naked body. Tears streamed down his face. He screamed a cry of loss and fury as he bent low over the silent form.

By the time the closest forensics man ran to the scene, the man had picked up the boy and held his head in his lap rocking gently back and forth.

"Don't touch me or I'll kill you," the man screamed.

The forensics man backed off. Chief Sanderson puffed up to the spot and knelt beside the pair.

"Easy, Lawson. Easy, man. We can't help your boy now. Too late for that. But we're going to find out who did this. Then you can yell at the killer."

Lawson Haskins sobbed as he held Willy. Slowly the rocking eased then stopped. Lawson gulped in huge breaths and his eyes lost some of their wild, crazy look. Gently he laid Willy back on the ground. Lawson looked up at the Sheriff and tried to talk but no real words came out. Guttural bellows of protest and agony spewed from his mouth. He shook his head, wiped his face with both hands, and looked back at Chief Sanderson.

"Who?" the one word came out jagged like a broken in windshield. The word rasped again.

"We don't know yet, Lawson. We'll find this killer and he'll pay for what he's done."

A late arriving ambulance crawled up to the spot, eased through a shallow ditch, and into the field until it was ten feet from the body.

"Lawson, we've got to take Willy to the county morgue. You understand?"

The father's head nodded an inch but he kept staring at his son's pale face. "Why? Why would some-body...." his words choked off.

Sanderson helped Lawson stand. "Officer Jones will drive you back to your place. He'll close up the store for you. Is that all right?"

Lawson kept staring at his son. "After..." he said motioning to the two medics who brought out a gurney and lowered it to the ground next to Willy.

"Yeah, Lawrence. You'll be able to see your boy at the county morgue."

The county detectives talked with the sheriff then one of them took Officer Jones's car keys to drive his Focus back to the Forest Glen Police Station.

By ten that morning, they knew a little more. Hardy, the Chief and one of the sheriff's detectives named Walter Grange sat in the Chief's office.

"So the ME said there were definite marks of an anal rape and signs of semen around the boy's penis. Probably his own. Also one laceration and lump on the side of Willy's head. So this was a sexual attack and not consensual."

"What did forensics find?" Hardy asked.

Deputy Sheriff Grange shook his head. "Not much.

Mostly garbage. There's a make out place a hundred yards up the road. High School kids mostly. Bunch of fast food paper, two used condoms, a black bra, and two tee shirts."

"No sign of the boy's clothes?" Chief Sanderson asked."

"Not a thread."

"So was he violated and strangled here, or was this just where he was discarded?" Hardy asked.

"No indications either way. So that's about all the good I can do you right now," the deputy said. "Sheriff said I should get back to work on my other case soon as I could."

"Thanks for the help," Chief Sanderson said. They waved and Deputy Grange left the room.

"I'll check the school and see if he was there yesterday," Hardy said. "Should have been a football practice day. I'll hang around and talk to the team. Somebody might have seen him get in a car. As I remember, he still doesn't have his driver's license."

"Good. We might get lucky. The forensic guys will check those condoms to see if there's any DNA on record anywhere."

"We couldn't get lucky and match the DNA with some pedophile on record," Hardy said. "I'm going out to the school and see what I can dig up." The chief waved and started putting together a file folder marked "Willy."

Out at Forest Glen High Hardy talked with the office people. Yes, Willy Haskins had attended all of his classes yesterday. The staff had heard about the death and it zapped all over school well before noon. There would be a special assembly tomorrow as a memorial for

Willy. Hardy thanked them and went to find the football coach.

Coach Chuck Brachman was visibly upset. His face was dawn and he kept shaking his h head as if he didn't believe it. He paced his small office in the boy's side of the gym, sat at his desk, got up, and paced again.

"Unbelievable. Just like that the boy is snatched and killed. Nothing like this ever happens in Forest Glen. Yes, he was at practice yesterday afternoon. I worked his ass off taking snaps and hitting the long down-and-outs, and post-routes. He was sharp. The kid had a scholarship ticket to half the colleges in the state including OSU and U of O. He was good and would get a lot better. Now he's dead and gone. Never thought much about that phrase before. Dead and gone. "

Hardy waited at the school for football practice to begin. Coach let him talk to the group for a minute before practice.

"So, if any of you have any idea what Willy did right after practice or later, come and see me. Coach said it was all right. We have to find out something here."

Later three boys came up. The first said Willy asked him for a ride home but the kid hadn't brought his car that day. The next boy said he had seen Willy leave the gym and start walking down School Lane that leads into town. The third boy said he passed Willy walking down School Lane, but his car was packed and no room for another rider.

Hardy took it down in his notebook. It was a start. Not much, but they knew now that he had walked away from school heading for town. He didn't walk the seven miles out to String Town Road. Somebody had picked him up, attacked him, and then murdered him. But who?

Hardy walked back to his cruiser. Another group of classes would be getting out soon. He'd wait and see if he could talk to anyone else about Willy. Somebody must have seen something.

ED RATHWOOD, 32, was the owner of Rathwood Fine Furniture, Forest Glen's only real furniture store. He had inherited it from his father when he was a junior at Forest Glen University. He wanted to be a doctor, but that wasn't to be. He had a competent staff of four who did most of the work and to his surprise he found himself quite talented at managing the business. Today he quit early, left the store in the capable hands of his manager, Uriah Condit, and drove his new Lexus out West Main to the edge of town where the Rathwood mansion sat well back in the wooded thirteen acre estate. He zapped open the locked front gate and drove into the four car garage. He went up stairs to the apartment once set up for the family driver. When the driver quit four year ago, Ed had taken over the space as his hide away, where he could get lost, seal himself away from the telephone, his cell phone, and all radio and TV signals.

He closed and locked the door then slumped on the

couch. The slanting roof on both sides had been closed in to form a room eight feet wide and almost twenty feet long. On the wall facing the couch he had installed a tack board and now he stared hard at it.

Center on the board hung a letterman's jacket in red and black with the prominent letters "FG" fastened to the front along with replicas of two footballs.

"Oh yes," Ed whispered. "Oh, yes, that was magnificent. It will be hard to top."

He trembled a moment as the surge of emotion blasted through him then he crumpled on the couch totally drained of strength and nervous energy.

He lay there for ten minutes going over and over the strike the night before. It had been perfect. Everything worked in sync, no accidental intrusions by strangers, no problems, and no mistakes.

He sat up, shook his head, and blinked. A miracle. He felt so alive, so relaxed, so enthused for life, so vibrant, powerful, and productive. The furies were all gone. The nagging voices had been stilled. The pressure that had been building for months had evaporated.

Now all he needed to do was go into the house and say hello and good bye to his mother. She became testy when he didn't at least acknowledge her once in a while. He lived there in the thirteen room mansion in his own apartment in the west wing. When he was home he usually took his meals there by himself.

His mother, Elmira, was 62, had a cook and a housekeeper who also served as her driver. She ran the mansion with the masterful grip of a General George Patton. So, he would say hello to his mother, chat a minute or two, head for Hillsboro seven miles toward

Portland, and then it would be off to his favorite restaurant, Arthurs. It would be the perfect ending to an exciting and excruciating fulfilling twenty four hours.

OFFICER HARDY JONES leaned on the front fender of his city patrol car with its black and white paint scheme. He had talked to three of the football players. He wondered if anyone else saw Willy Haskins walking up School Lane the day before. The kids who came out of school from the last class seemed to know why he was there. A few waved. He said hi to three or four he knew. Then a girl came up and frowned. She almost went by, then stopped, and walked up to him.

"You trying to find out who killed Willy?"

"Yes, Miss. I am. Did you see him after school yesterday?"

She hesitated. She was slender, tall, maybe a volley-ball player. She frowned and nodded.

"I stayed late in the library and when I came out, I saw Willy walking ahead of me. I knew it was him. He has a little swagger when he walks. He was about a block away." She nodded. "Yes, a block ahead but I knew it was him."

"What happened then?"

"Oh, this old car came along. It was probably twenty years old, had rust spots, and two or three colors of paint. The passenger's side door was a different color than the rest."

"It went right past you??"

"Yes and when it came near Willy he turned and held out his thumb, hitch hiking. The car stopped. They must have talked a bit, then Willy got in, and the car drove away."

Hardy felt a surge of excitement. A real lead. He took a quick breath and asked the vital question. "Did you get the license number?"

"No. No reason I should. But thinking back, I don't remember seeing a license plate on the back."

Hardy had out his notebook and wrote quickly. "Good, you remembered a lot. Now, is there anything else about the car that you can think of? Like a logo that showed what make it was? Did you see who was driving? Anything else?"

"Thought I told you. A man was driving. Not too old, but no kid. Maybe thirty or so."

"Any idea what make of car?"

"Not a clue. My little brother could have told you. I don't know one from the other."

"Were the windows tinted?"

"No, but there were four doors. The passenger's side window was rolled down all the way."

"Good. Now about the driver. Was he white, Hispanic or, black?"

"Oh, he was white, no beard that I saw. Seems like his hair was dark."

"Miss, could I have your name? You've been most helpful."

Her name was Beth Mason. Hardy gave her his card and asked her to call if she remembered anything else about the car or the driver. He waited another half hour, but no one else came to talk. He left the circular drive in front of the office and hurried back to the station. Now they had a little bit more to work with.

Five minutes later when Hardy came in the front door of the station, Chief Sanderson waved him into his office

"Got some news from the forensic guys. Guess what? One of them went back out there with a metal detector and came up with two dollars' worth of change, three silverware forks, and a fraternity pin."

"College kids all over that place after dark," Hardy said.

"This is a local frat, the Gamma Sigma fraternity. They have a small house off Forest Glen campus. I sent Young over there to ask around, see what he can find out. Like maybe somebody lost a pin last night?" Bob Young was the other day cop on duty.

"Hope it helps. I've got something new from the high school." He took out his notebook and told the chief everything he had picked up from Beth. The chief took notes as fast as he could write.

"Oh, yeah, Jones. You did good. This is a real break. All we need to do is find that beat up old sedan..."

"Chief, I've been driving these streets for six years, and I watch the cars. I've never seen a rig that looks anything like the way Beth described it."

"Now we all watch harder. It might be new to town, or maybe somebody is repainting it. We've got something solid to go on."

"And we know it was a man in his thirties," Hardy

said. "Cuts our list of possible Forest Glen suspects down to maybe three or four hundred."

The chief tapped a pen on his desk pad. "How many RSO's we have in the county? Know we have some."

"Registered Sex Offenders," Hardy said. "I can't remember the last one. We had one last year, the guy fondling that little girl. But he went away for three to five. I'll call the sheriff's office. They have the map with locations."

Ten minutes later Hardy had the figure and the addresses of three RSO's in and around Forest Glen. He didn't know any of them.

"Get on them. Talk to all three today and check for alibis. Maybe we'll turn up something."

Twenty minutes later Hardy spoke with Tom Fulton's wife.

"I know why you're here and Tom didn't have anything to do with it. He was at home after supper from six to midnight when we went to bed."

Tom was at work at the Forest Garage. Hardy drove there. Tom pulled greasy plastic gloves off, threw them away, and then glared at Hardy.

"Wondered when you would be around. You're slow this time. No, I didn't have anything to do with Willy's murder. I was home all evening and night. Ask my wife."

"Wives don't make good witnesses in court," Hardy said. "Anybody else see you?"

Tom paused. "Yeah, matter of fact. My next door neighbor came over to borrow my power screwdriver. That was maybe nine thirty." Tom waved. "Yeah you want his name. He's Bob Hemphil and he works at the

Forest Glen National Bank. Now I've got a tune-up to finish or the boss will take my hide off."

"Okay, Tom. If you hear anything, let me know." Hardy gave him a card and headed for the bank. Tom was pissed which was natural. But he looked clean. A wife and a neighbor made a pretty good alibi. Now he had two more to find. If he was lucky he'd be done before midnight.

ED HAD NEVER LIKED ANIMALS. That summer that he was six he was in his yard playing with matches. He had found a whole box of wooden kitchen matches and hidden them in his secret spot in the garage. It was summer and he was bored. Then Charlie from down the street came over to play. Ed told his mother he and Charlie would be playing Indians in the back woods.

He took along the box of matches to show off.

In the woods, he grinned at Charlie. "Bet you don't know what I have."

"A snake maybe a frog?"

"No dummy. A whole box of matches."

"Wowie. A boxful. Your mom would skin you."

"She won't know. Hey, we could have a bonfire."

"Naw, we might burn down the woods. My Dad is a fireman."

"Yea I forgot that. Hey, look. That old cat that's been hanging around."

"Can we pet her?"

"If you want to. She's tame."

Charlie picked up the cat and stroked its patchy dark fur. It looked up and purred. Ed scowled.

"I hate cats," Ed said.

"Even this old one? Listen to her purr."

"I know what we can do. You hold her real tight and I'll scare her with a lighted match."

"Don't hurt her."

Ed took out two matches and went to the side of Charlie. The old cat lay in his arms, purring away.

"Don't hurt her," Charlie said.

"Naw, won't." Ed struck the matches together across the box's rough surface. The matches flared into a bright flame and he pushed the fire midway in the cat's long tail. The fur caught fire and raced along the tail.

The animal let out a screeching howl, clawed away from Charlie, and hit the ground running around the small clearing in a circle bleating in fury and pain.

"Why you do that?" Charlie yelled.

Ed held his box of matches and laughed so hard he couldn't stop. "Look at that dumb old cat with its tail on fire. Boy, I bet she will remember this day."

Charlie ran after the cat but couldn't catch it. He gave up and came back and slugged Ed on the shoulder.

"You did that on purpose. I hate you. Never going to play with you again." Charlie turned and walked quickly back past the house and to the street.

Ed could still see the cat. The fire had gone out and half the hair on its tail had burned off.

He watched the cat a little more until it vanished in the brush and trees. Then he went back to the garage and hid the matches in his secret spot. Never could tell when he might need them again. He wondered if he had tied up the cat first if all the fur on its whole body would have burned off. He nodded. It was something he would try the next time he could catch a cat.

BOB YOUNG STOPPED at the three story house on Fifth Avenue that had been a small hospital at one time. Now it was the Gamma Sigma fraternity house. Not big or fancy, but a hangout the Gammas loved. Young went up the wooden steps and was almost run over by a kid barreling out the front door. He stopped and saluted.

"Yes sir, officer sir. You bet. What can Gamma Sigma do for you this fine day?" Young figured the kid wasn't shaving yet so probably a freshman. The kid squinted up at Young who was six feet two.

"I need to talk to your president or one of your officers. Is anyone home?"

"Our veep is here. You'll better come inside to wait. I'll have to pry him away from his lap top."

"Inside will be fine."

Five minutes later a short black kid with bulging upper body muscles came into the living room and held out his hand.

"I'm Justin. How can Gamma Sigma serve Forest Glen's finest this morning?"

"We need to talk to your man who lost his frat pin during the past two or three days."

"Yeah we lose those frigging pins all the time. The clasps on them are faulty. We bitched to the maker but so far no recourse. Lost his pin? Jeez, Officer, that could be any one of eight or ten guys. Like I said..."

"Let's cut down the time frame to anyone who lost his pin last night. That should shorten the list."

"Uh, yes. Cut down the list. Most of our guys are in class right now. I'll check the men who are here and give you a quick report."

"Good, this is an urgent situation."

"Be right with you. You want a beer while you wait? Oh, no, I forgot you're on duty." Just turned and ran up a flight of open stairs.

Ten minutes later, Justin was back. "Hey, you're in luck. Found two culprits for you. Wimpy and Carl are putting on some clothes and will be right down."

When they came, Justin did the introductions

"This is Wimp. Yeah, he's a little heavy but you should hear the way he wails. Best baritone on campus."

"Wimpy how did you lose your pin?"

"Damndedst thing. Some little blonde bitch reached inside my shirt, undid the clasp, and ran away with my pin. Those suckers cost forty bucks now."

Officer Young thanked Wimpy and excused him. Carl had slipped into the room while Wimpy talked. He was older, maybe a senior, with red hair, slim with pale skin, and shifting green eyes.

"Carl, say hello to the nice officer," Justin said. Carl nodded.

Young asked how he lost his pin.

"Don't know where or when. It wasn't there when I sobered up this morning."

"You own a car?"

"Yeah, a Beamer."

Justin chuckled. "Oh, yeah. His folks are loaded with old money."

"Carl, did you drive last night?"

"Not that I know of. Look, I've got to study. This test is coming up and if I don't..."

Officer Young waved him away. When Carl left, Young asked Justin to get Carl's license number and his full name. Then he gave Justin his card. "If you come up with any good ideas who else lost a pin, give me a call."

"Will do. What's this all about?"

"I can't tell you, but it's serious. Give me any names you have before eight tonight at that number."

Back at the station he told the chief what he had learned. The Chief grunted.

"Put it in your report. We think the car may have been a twenty year old beat up jalopy."

HARDY JONES WASN'T HAVING MUCH BETTER luck than he had with the other RSO's. The banker backed up the mechanic. He worked on the second name, Nate Vuysteke. His last known was a run-down boarding house on Second Street. He knew the place. Five would get you a thousand that Nate didn't live there anymore. Hardy talked with the manager who snorted.

"Hey, if you find him you get the fifty bucks he owes me for back rent. He took off in the middle of the night two months ago. I haven't seen the slob sine."

Hardy thanked the manager, went back to his squad car, and the next name on his list. Orlando Paul. Hardy remembered him. He was a nasty dude who served two years for molesting a little girl. He was on three years' probation. A blonde woman about thirty answered the door a t the duplex.

She was slender, wore short shorts, a tight revealing tee shirt, and a smile.

"Yeah, just like he said. Knew you would be coming around. He ain't here. Didn't want to talk to you. I don't know where he went. Said he'd be gone for a week or so."

"What's he driving?"

"His beat-up old Dodge. Most of it's a Dodge. I told him to get a paint job but he didn't. It's about six different shades."

"Two or four doors?"

"Hey, you think I'm a mechanic or something? Yeah, okay, four doors."

"Thanks. When you hear from him, tell him we want to talk to him, but it's just routine. He'll understand."

"Oh, yeah, understand." She looked at him again. "Hey, you got half an hour to waste? Why not come in and sit a spell." She swung the screen door open and pushed out her chest.

"Bet we could figure out something interesting to do. Just the two of us."

Hardy closed his note book, touched his hat, and hurried back down the sidewalk to his patrol car. Before he got to his car his cell phone sang its little song. He grabbed it.

"Yeah, Chief?"

"We have a small problem. You best be getting back to the station as soon as you can make it."

"I'm moving, Chief." Hardy frowned. The Chief almost never called on the cell phone unless it was something important. He wanted to hit the siren as he drove but didn't. What had the Chief so uptight?

6

KING BRODERSON WAS a rough and rugged character around town who ran the Broderson's Grocery. For the past year he had been planning and working deals that would set him up to finance a large shopping center just east of town called the

Broderson Shopping Center with the Broderson Super Store as the key. He had already bought three houses in the area, a twenty acre small farm, and had two more parcels in escrow. He was almost ready to start construction. The Forest Glen Chamber of Commerce had come out against the project. Said it would kill the downtown merchants. King Broderson snorted and said "Tough. It's every merchant for himself."

His whole name was Emmet King Broderson, but few people knew about the Emmet part. He had been King since high school. He was a huge supporter of the Forest Glen Tigers and had even signed up Willy Haskins to be the spokesman for his store, just as soon as he graduated from college. King liked to look ahead. He didn't even know if it was legal or not but had Willy's father sign the same agreement just in case. Now the kid was dead and gone. Who would want to kill a kid like that? Could be some psycho pedophile or maybe a homo rape that got out of hand. He'd let the cops figure it out. He had enough problems. That made him think about Coach Brachman. King had seen every high school home game and nobody had taken any snaps from center during a game but Willy. Coach must be tearing his jersey off trying to find a new quarterback.

Now he had a new problem with the shopping center. Some weirdo group in town had filed a lawsuit against him claiming that he didn't have the proper environmental study made on the site and claiming that construction would bring dangerous operations to the area. It was a half mile from a middle school and if completed would bring crippling and polluting traffic to that low profile area. His lawyer was fighting it but you never could tell.

He had verbal commitments from two other merchants who would rent space in the Shopping Center if he would build to suit. One of them was Ed Rathwood and the Rathwood Fine Furniture store.

King sat at his small desk at the back of his modest grocery store and thought about the future. He'd had experts judge the situation. Forest Glen was growing. The city limits were expanding. Modest new sub divisions of twenty to thirty houses were going up. There was no large franchise grocery outlet in town or within seven miles.

He would copy some of the Von's, Safeway's, and Albertson's approaches, and also mix it up with the Wal-Mart system, with everything that a home owner needed. It could be a gold mine.

His lawyer was working on finding out the names of those behind the suit. They were asking for a temporary restraining order to prevent him from starting construction in three weeks. He was ready to go. Had the drawings all dome and approved by the county. The contractor was waiting for the start signal. Now this lawsuit.

He called Ed with a sudden thought. The man was in.

"Hey, Ed, King. You know anything about the bunch behind this lawsuit I I've got on the shopping center?"

"Haven't heard a whistle, King. Only thing I know is that some outfit in Portland is handling the legal end."

"Damn buzzards are out looking for carrion. You're still with me on that store right beside mine?"

"Right. Gonna cost me a ton of cash to move, but it's about time Forest Glen had a center like this. Proud of you to get it moving."

"Yeah, unless it's stopped. Hey, what we gonna do for a new quarterback?"

"Brachman hasn't had to use a backup so far this season. Puts him in a real hole. He must be sweating bundles of bullets."

"Guess we'll find out Friday night. So, thanks. I just wanted to check with you on the shopping center. Judge said he'd hear arguments on Thursday."

"Who's your lawyer?"

"Loophole. Used him for years. If he can't find some

legal way around it, he'll find some loophole in the law. What he says anyway. Hey, I've got to go. Good talking with you."

"Yeah. Hang in there on that Thursday talk with the judge."

They hung up.

7

OFFICER HARDY JONES parked in the reserved spot at the Forest Glen Police station and hurried inside. Chief Sanderson waved Young and Hardy into his office and then settled in his chair behind his modest desk.

"We may have a break. Don't know for sure, but it's worth a good long look. Had a call from Elmer Foley, principal at the high school. It may be a he said she said. But we're going to see how it plays out.

"Two months ago Willy Haskins had been bragging to his buddies about how a teacher had come on to him and exposed herself to him in a classroom. She suggested that they have sex right there right then. The principal said when he heard the same story from two boys about the incident, he called Willy into his office and they talked it out. He was adamant that this female teacher had offered him sex in her classroom. He said she exposed her breasts to him. The principal told him flat out to stop talking about it around school or anywhere else or he'd be thrown off the team. That did it for Willy.

"The principal said he'd had a talk with the teacher involved and she said it was absolutely false. She said she'd had stories told about her before. She assured him she had no sexual fantasies about teen age boys. She said they were so immature that they were totally asexual as far she was concerned. He said that was the end of it. But now, with what happened to Willy, he thought he should come forward."

The chief looked at his two patrolmen. "So, what do you men think about this?"

Young shook his head. "Doesn't make much sense to me. Seventeen year old hormones go wild. If he'd had the chance he would have jumped her. So why would he turn her in?"

Hardy Jones rubbed his face with his right hand. "Got to be something there. We at least have to talk to the teacher, get her side of it. Willy can't defend himself, but we still have to talk to her."

"I agree," the Chief said. "She's due here at three-thirty today. I want both of you here. We'll listen to what she has to say then ask her questions."

"I thought Willy was a homosexual kill," Jones said. "But nothing at the scene could confirm that. A woman could have done him in. If the autopsy shows alcohol in his blood, it would have been easy for a woman to do it. Probably have sex with him, then if he threatened to expose her, she could have hit him with something, knocked him out, and then strangled him."

"Could have been," Chief Sanderson said. "We should have the coroner's report tomorrow about noon." The meeting broke up. Hardy went back to the squad room and found the newspaper picture of Willy Haskins. He thumb tacked it to the big bulletin board. On a 3 x 5 card he wrote Willy's name and put that over the picture. Then he sat down and made a list on his lap top about what they knew concerning Willy's demise.

. Date of death: 9-24-14
. Time of death: 10 PM to 3 AM
. A homicide
. Seen getting in an old grungy car after practice
. Cause of death: strangulation
. Found naked. Clothes missing
. No tire tracks at the scene
. Gamma Sigma frat pin at scene
. Willy had complained about sexual advance by teacher
. Star quarterback for FG Tigers
. Could have been woman killer

He printed it out and tacked the list under Willy's picture. If these were the parts to a puzzle, they sure weren't fitting together. They needed much more. Maybe the autopsy report would tell them something new. Maybe.

A half-hour later, Hardy answered a call from dispatch about a collision on Market Street. Two women had a fender bender. No one hurt. He talked to them for fifteen minutes. He took accident reports from both and talked them into calling their insurance companies and letting them handle the details of any settlement. By the time the women parted, they were almost friends. It was just past three-thirty when Hardy walked into the conference room. The Chief and Young were already there as well as the guest of honor, Miss

Madelyn Tesser, 28, blonde, slender, and what Hardy called well-endowed.

"Miss Tesser, this is Officer Jones. He'll be sitting in on our talk."

"I really don't see how I can help you..."

The Chief held up his hand. "Let's see how it turns out. Now, as I suggested, I want you to tell us exactly what happened a couple of months ago when Willy Haskins stayed in your room after the other students had left."

"Well, all right. I teach English. We were in a composition unit and it was going well. Some of the kids could actually write complete sentences. I looked up from grading a paper and Willy stood in front of my desk in a kind of show off slouch he had. I asked him what he wanted and he laughed.

"'Woman, you know what I want,' he said.

"He then rubbed his crotch. I jumped up and yelled at him to leave the room at once. He laughed again and said it was a shame that all my good stuff was going to waste, not getting screwed. Those were the words he used."

"You didn't encourage him in any way?" Hardy asked.

"No I did not. All my life I've had trouble with men and boys who think just because I have large breasts that I'm ready to tear off my clothes for them. It's been hard."

"What happened next?" The Chief asked.

"I threw my dictionary at him. It's a big one and it hit his right arm. He swore at me, used filthy language, and screamed I might have hurt his passing arm. I pointed toward the door and picked up my house phone to call security. I hit the three buttons and said: Security? This is room 204. I have a problem with a student. By the time I said it he had run out the door and I didn't see him again for three class sessions."

"You reported this to the vice principal?" Young asked.

She hesitated. "Well, no. I didn't see what good it would do. If I reported every sexual harassment I get, the Veep would have a file for me an inch thick. It just isn't fair."

"Did he made any advances to you after that?" the Chief asked.

She shook her head. "No, he dropped my class and took a reading class instead for his English requirement."

"How do you feel about Willy's death?" Hardy asked.

She sighed and shook her head. "So sad. He was a good football player. My boyfriend says he would have got a four year scholarship at Oregon State and after graduating there he'd be drafted by the pros. He was that good. Now that's all wasted. He didn't deserve to be murdered."

The Chief looked at Jones who shook his head. "All right, Miss Tesser, I think we're done here unless you have something else to add."

She frowned. "No, I don't think so. The kids at school say it was a homosexual killing. I wouldn't know. I'm just so sorry that it happened. Now, I hope that this is the end of it for me. I had no involvement. I know of no one who did. Period."

The Chief stood. The patrolmen stood. Then the

tall, blonde, beautiful school teacher got up, nodded to the chief, and walked out the front door.

The Chief looked at his men. "So?"

"Yes, they are large sized," Young said.

"If we can prove it was a woman, then she is a suspect," Hardy said. "First we get that autopsy report."

IT WAS JUST after one-thirty a.m. when Hardy's phone blasted him wide awake. He grabbed it and recognized the automated call to all Forest Glen Volunteer Firemen.

"Fire call," he told Cindy and grabbed his pants and shoes. It took him two more minutes to finish dressing and six minutes to drive the three miles to the small fire station. Four volunteers were there ahead of him. They pulled on their firefighting suits and gear and lunged for the town's one pamper fire engine that rolled toward the big doors.

"Where at?" Hardy asked the man beside him.

"The Broderson Grocery, dispatch said somebody caught it early."

"Hope so."

It was only two minutes to the grocery store in downtown Forest Glen half a block down from Pacific Avenue and Main. Flames gushed from the front door of the fifty foot wide building,

They saw that it was a small fire and used a heavy mist nozzle knocking down the flames in five minutes. Then Hardy got a notebook from the engine and started making out a report. The door had glass windows on the top half. The glass had been broken inward in two places. When it cooled down enough Hardy found a broken glass jar just inside the door. He could smell gasoline on the fragments. He estimated the damage just as Broderson showed up swearing, naming names, and furious as a de-clawed bob cat.

"Damn right I know who did this. Bunch who are trying to stop me from putting up the shopping center. They told me they won't stop fighting. This has to be them. Bastards. Hope you can get some prints. All I need is one, just one of the sonsofbitches."

Eight volunteers had answered the call. Now they pulled out charred wood and some wet and soggy grocery items. They had kept the water damage to a minimum. Within an hour they had the place cleaned up and Broderson had nailed plywood over the ruined front door. They left with Broderson sitting in a chair by the outside of the front door with a double barreled shotgun across his knees.

"Just hope to hell they come back and try again," Broderson said. "Hey Hardy, no law broken here. I'm out duck hunting and this is my legal shotgun."

Hardy waved at him and caught the big yellow engine just as it pulled out. It would take them another hour to clean up the rig .What the hell he didn't really want to get any more sleep tonight anyway.

The next morning an assistant Medical Examiner drove the autopsy report over the seven miles from Hillsboro. He arrived at eleven fifteen and Hardy had just reported in for the day shift. He had come home from the fire about three a.m. and Cindy let him sleep in until ten. The ME didn't wait for questions. He left the file folder and drove away.

Chief Sanderson read it then showed it to Hardy. Young was out on a call. Hardy read it quickly and then went through it slowly. He walked into the chief's office and waited until the top cop looked up.

"So?"

"Evidence of anal penetration but no semen deposited. So it was a homosexual killing. They found evidence of tearing and bruising in Willy's mouth and throat, which could indicate fellatio. Then later it says particles of latex such as used in condoms were found in the throat area." Hardy looked up. "So that ties it down as a homosexual rape murder. Should rule out our idea of a woman killer. Miss Big Boobs teacher is cleared."

"He also indicated several bruises on Willy's arms and the laceration on his head," the chief said. "I'd guess that means that Willy put up a fight. Also there were two broken fingers on his right hand. Wonder what the other guy looks like?"

"If we find him in time. The final report lists cause of death as strangulation." The chief gave a small soundless groan. This was about what he was afraid the ME would find. Which put them in the same hole as before. No evidence, no witnesses, and for sure no suspects.

Hardy put the report back in the file folder and placed it on the Chief's desk.

"Spit it out, Hardy. Every time you get that hang dog look you are coming up with some kind of wild notions."

"Yeah, didn't know I was so easy to read. Okay, I'm still not sure about that teacher. Miss Tesser. Something doesn't ring true about her. She told a good story but I had a feeling she was putting on a show for us. Maybe she was a drama minor in college when she got her teaching certificate."

"What did she do wrong?"

"Nothing. That's part of what bothers me. She had all of the answers. She covered all the bases. She had back up for her back up and covered her ass at all times."

"You're serious. What more can we do?"

"I want to nose around the school a little. I've got a kid out there who owes me. I gave him a warning when I could have nailed him with a ticket. He might know something about Miss Tesser we don't. Or he might know some boys who have been in her pants. Worth a try. All on a hush, hush basis. Can I try it?"

"Sure. On your own time and out of uniform. Okay?"

"Only way, Chief. Now how in hell do we get something on this killer?"

"Talk to forensics at County. Maybe they've come up with prints from the garbage they picked up. Want them to use a fine tooth microscope on that junk."

"I'm on it."

Deputy Alpone in forensics groaned when Hardy identified himself on the phone.

"Damn, I was afraid you were going to call, been over all the stuff from that kill site. Three times we worked it. We found six prints good enough to try for a match. The state lab said no matches on five. We had a hit on the last one and he's local. Only trouble is, we sent him to prison for three to five two months ago for burglary."

"So we're still nowhere."

"Maybe not. I was in vice for a while. Seems like

some of the RSO's like to get out of town for their little parties. You're seven clicks down the road. You want our list of RSO's?"

"How many you have?"

"Only three who like teen age boys. Half a dozen more who go for little girls, and then about twenty for indecent exposure. Penis bragging I call it."

"Hey, email me the three homos. Send it to rjones77@prc.com. We might give them a shot and see how they react. Sooner the better."

"I'll get right on the computer. Take care."

They hung up and Hardy told the chief about the fruits of his call.

"Three more shots," the chief said. "Get on those as soon as you get the names."

That afternoon Hardy had to patrol Fifth Street to satisfy a group of residents who had complained to the mayor about speeders going up to fifty miles an hour. He stopped one little old lady driving a new Cadillac who had no idea she was doing forty five mph in a twenty five mile zone. He wrote her up and sent her on her way. The rest of the hour long patrol was without incident.

He checked twice with the dispatcher but no email had come in for him from the county sheriff. Instead she sent him out to a family dispute on Pacific Highway just in the city limits. A screaming, yelling, and pot throwing argument had worked its way to the front lawn where the wife had turned the garden hose on the man and he had tackled her just as Hardy drove up. He gave the siren a couple of turns and the wrestlers stopped and watched him park.

"Damn woman should be locked up," the man

bellowed. "She came at me with a foot long butcher knife."

"That was after he threatened me with his shotgun," the woman screeched and swung the hose around again, soaking her husband and Hardy in the process. Hardy ran and turned off the water then confronted the pair.

"You look like a drowning caribou," the woman said to her husband.

He laughed. "You look like the loser in a wet tee shirt contest," he said.

They both laughed.

Hardy waited. Sometimes that worked best. The woman frowned, pushed long dark hair off her face, and looked thoughtful. "You remember what we were arguing about?"

He snorted. "Hell no. Not the hint of an idea." He shook his head. "If you get cleaned up and change into some dry clothes I'll take you out to dinner."

"Better not be Taco Bell."

"Hell no. Some place classy, maybe McDonalds." They both laughed and ignored Hardy as they walked arm and arm into the modest house.

Hardy went back to his cruiser, reported the family dispute settled, and was sent to an injury crash on Main Street. Officer Young was already there, so Hardy directed traffic around the T-bone collision on Main and First Street. The ambulance guys loaded a woman on a gurney and into the rig.

Back at the station, the email came through from the Sheriff's Office just before five o'clock. He was due off at five today. Some days they pulled twelve hour shifts but they didn't advertise it. So for four hours there was only one officer on duty. He looked at the list of names and addresses of the RSO's all in Hillsboro. Hardy put the list on his desk with a stapler holding it down. It was his first call in the morning. He wasn't sure when he would get out to the high school kids.

Joanie, the dispatcher, said King Broderson had filed a report of an arson fire. The chief had sent it on to the District Attorney in Hillsboro.

Hardy looked forward to a long night's catch up sleep. In the morning he'd attack Hillsboro and the three Registered Sex Offenders. He might get lucky.

8

CHARLOTTE ALBERTS REMEMBERED what her mother had said. It was too dangerous to walk through this end of the park on her way to and from school. Hell, she was thirteen. She'd had the sex education classes. She even took that woman self-defense class and learned how to stomp on a man's foot and kick him right in the balls. She giggled. That word always sounded so dirty to her. "Balls," she said out loud then giggled again.

She stopped part way through the park that was half filled with tall Douglas fir trees and a lot of native brush and smaller trees. Did she hear something behind her? She took a few more steps then glanced over her shoulder. Yeah, nothing and nobody on the trail to the rear. She was getting to be a scaredy cat. Charlotte turned around and gasped. She wanted to scream but nothing came out of her mouth.

Less than three feet in front of her stood a tall naked man holding a knife with blood dripping off it. Her feet seemed frozen to the ground. She dropped her books, whirled to run, but he was too quick. He grabbed her arm and swung her around.

"Stay absolutely quiet, Charlotte, or I'll slit your throat." His voice was soft, almost melodious as his grip on her arm tightened. "It won't be the first blood I've drawn today." His empty hand stabbed over her mouth shutting off any sound she could make. He picked her up like she was a big stuffed toy and growled at her.

"Remember, just one little peep out of you and I'll slit you gizzard to gander, depending where your gander is." He chuckled at his own joke and carried her rapidly through some brush into a part of the park where Charlotte had never been. Half way into the thicket he stopped, stood her up, and picked up a folded costume from beside a tree. He pulled on what she saw was a long black robe. Then he stood beside her and closed the black robe around them both covering her completely. He picked her up and walked to the side of the park where there were no houses facing it.

Charlotte's head was covered so she couldn't tell what was happening. He carried her across the last few yards of the park and stepped into a minivan that had the sliding door open. He laid her on the rear seat, tied a gag around her mouth, and bound her hands and feet with stout cord. He covered her except her head with a red and black blanket then stood back and smiled.

"Part one a total success, small one. Wouldn't you agree?"

She glared at him but couldn't answer. He still had the black robe on. She felt a chill deep in her bones. Terror wasn't strong enough for what flooded over her. Her mother had been right about the park. Damn. What could she do now? Maybe he would just....rape her and let her go. Silent tears ran down her cheeks where she lay under the blanket. A chill tore through her and she tried to cry out but the gag muffled it into a whimper. Charlotte Alberts closed her eyes and a dread she had never known closed in around her. She was going to die, she knew it for certain. Today was going to be the last day of her life.

In the van's driver seat, the tall man in the black robe drove carefully. Now would not be a good time to be stopped by a cop for some traffic violation. He drove out of the small town in the direction of the hills to the west which were the beginnings of the Coast Range of mountains. He knew precisely where he was going. He had scouted out the location one afternoon a month ago. He soon left a paved road that had taken him ten miles into the hills and turned into a gravel road that wound upward past a small farm, a prune orchard, and then into a deserted farm house at the end of the road that had become little more than a double track with grass and weeds growing in the center. He drove the minivan around to the side of the dilapidated structure where it couldn't be seen from the road.

He turned off the engine then pulled the blanket down so Charlotte would look at him.

"There now, that wasn't so bad, was it? Of course not. Now, Charlotte, we are going to have some rules. First I'll take off your gag, if you promise me that you'll scream your head off. Right, scream all you want to. You see no one will hear you. The closest farm house is 6.4 miles away. Not a living human being anywhere around." He took the gag off and sat her up on the van's rear seat.

Charlotte didn't scream.

He lifted his brows. "No scream? Good. Now sit still while I take some things inside. We might as well be comfortable, right?"

"Who are you? What are you going to do to me?"

He smiled and it angered her more.

"Don't smile at me, you weirdo. I've heard all about men like you. Can't get it by themselves, so they kidnap girls. Makes you a poor excuse of a man, doesn't it?"

He slapped her hard across her face. She fell to the side and lay there, glaring at him.

"If you want a name, you can call me Satan, a good Old Testament name you must have heard." He picked up a box and two blankets and opened the van's sliding door.

She watched him go and tried to untie her hands but she couldn't. More tears came.

A moment later he was back, untied her ankles, and sat her up. He helped her out of the van and down a dirt walkway to a sagging door. For the first time she noticed that it was almost dark. He pushed her into the building and she saw he had lit a lantern that gave off a pale yellow light.

Instead of trembling, she looked around. An old mattress lay against the far wall. He had thrown the blankets on top of it. There was one folding metal chair but no other furniture.

"High school kids come up here to make out, shoot up, and have beer parties," the tall man said. "I cleaned it up." He spread out the two blankets on the bed then pushed her down on them. She sat up her eyes wide with terror, her glance darting around the shack.

"Charlotte, I've been watching you. Every day you cut through the park on your way home from school.

You're thirteen, maybe fourteen, and you have larger breasts than most girls your age. I'm a tit man. I admit it. So I chose you. You're one of the chosen, Charlotte."

She screamed. The sound came like a roaring rock concert climax, bouncing off the walls, penetrating every corner of the tumbled down structure. When she stopped she began crying again.

The man in the black robe sat down beside her. "That was good. Get it out of your system. Then it won't interrupt anything later." He reached over and started to unbutton her white blouse.

"No!" she shouted swinging her still tied hands at him.

"Yes," he said, swatting down her hands and ripping off the buttons on her blouse. It sagged open, showing her pink bra.

"I get tired of older women. Always want things their way. Telling me what they like and what turns them on. Some say, 'Oh I never do it that way.' If I insist they get all uptight and angry. When I want it, I want it the way I want it, and not a lot of silly talk from some damn stupid tiny-titted woman." He used a knife to slice through the center of her bra and push the cups aside.

"Oh, yes, Charlotte. What nice ones. You must be proud of them. So fresh and young and up-thrust just the way I like them. Beautiful breasts."

Charlotte screamed as he fondled her breasts, his hands rough and demanding. She screamed again and again. The tall man laughed then slapped her until she quieted.

"The screaming was supposed to be over. Now

settle down. I'm sure some boy has petted your breasts, probably fucked you too."

"No, never. Never. Nobody ever." She couldn't stop shivering. Her teeth chattered and her eyes showed the depths of her fear.

"Hey, Charlotte. You don't have to lie about it. Not anymore. Let me cut off the rest of your clothes—then I can see you all naked and beautiful. After that I'll take off my robe and you can see me, too." He laughed softly. "You said never? You've never made love with some horny high school boy. Well, well, a virgin. I'm getting more than I counted on. This is going to be a night to remember."

JUST AFTER EIGHT o'clock that same evening, Frank Alberts barged into the Forest Glen Police department office. Sweat beaded his forehead. His face was red and he had the look of a furious cougar.

"My little girl is missing," he shouted. "She's always home by two-thirty. She's been missing for over five hours. You've got to find her."

Officer Karl Easter took out a form and pushed it in front of the frightened man.

"Yes sir. Put down her name and age, fill in the blanks. We'll need to know what she was wearing, who her friends are..."

"We've called all her friends. Nobody has seen her since school let out. Something terrible has happened to her. How can we find her?"

Officer Easter grabbed the phone and called the Chief.

"That's all I know. No chance she's a runaway. Should I call in the rest of the guys?"

"Right, Easter, and I'll be there in ten minutes. Hard to find anything at night, but we can get a start. Make those calls."

Four hours later the five officers met back at the station. They had talked with Charlotte's mother who told them the usual route her daughter used to walk to school which was about a mile away.

Mrs. Alberts was in her thirties, a little heavy with now tousled brown hair. She had been crying. She had looked up at Officer Hardy Jones.

"Sometimes she walks through the park the south end. Says it saves her fifteen minutes. I told her not to. It can be a dangerous place."

They had found her books and backpack scattered just off the walking trail through the park about midnight.

"We'll call this off until daylight," Chief Sanderson said. "Be here at six thirty and we'll get some volunteers to scour the park and that whole area. We might get lucky."

At daylight the Chief and twenty volunteers combed through the park's five acres, digging into every shrub, thicket, and any place where a body could be hidden.

Nothing.

Word spread fast in the small town and by noon they had fifty volunteers. They worked a two block wide swath along the route Charlotte usually took all the way to the high school.

Nothing.

The story hit the *Oregonian* newspaper in Portland

and a group from the state Search and Rescue Team would come the next day to assist. An expert on missing children would fly in from Seattle. The small town of about three thousand people was on edge. More mothers drove their children to school and picked them up. Every door in town was locked tight day and night.

Chief Sanderson was puzzled. It was the first missing child case in town that they hadn't solved within a few hours. They had been one runaway and two kids staying at a friend's house after school and not telling their mothers.

THE THIRD DAY they had a break. A farmer called in about noon.

"Chief Sanderson?"

"Right. Who is this?"

"Homer Long. Have a little farm up west of town. I think I found Charlotte Alberts."

9

HIS MOTHER HAD MADE him watch. Edward Rathwood was eight at the time. He remembered that because they had celebrated his birthday at the lake. His mother hated the lake even though the cabin was new, modern, and comfortable.

She called him to the back yard and showed him the mongrel dog she had tied to a small tree.

"Little devil was into the garbage cans again, so I caught him. Now he gets what he deserves." She untied the rope from the tree and dragged the twenty pound animal back into the brush behind the cabin.

"Edward, you need to watch this so you don't grow up to be a wimp. I can't stand weak men. Your father, there is a strong one. Smart, too."

His dad had gone fishing. Again. Edward was starting to hate the taste of fish. Three nights running they had baked rainbow trout for dinner.

"An animal like this doesn't deserve to live," his mother said. She tied the end of the rope to a small tree and walked up to the brown haired dog. Its eyes glowed with what could have been fear or terror.

She took a ten-inch long butcher knife from her apron pocket, stepped up to the dog, and stabbed it deeply in the side.

The dog screeched in agony and fell to one side. His mother knelt beside the animal, slit its throat with the knife, then stabbed it a dozen more times. Edward dropped to the ground but couldn't tear his gaze away from the dying dog.

That was when he heard his mother laughing. He'd never heard her laugh that way before. A high piercing sound that drilled through his head. He knew he would never forget it.

When the dog made its last shiver and lay still, his mother untied the rope from around its neck and dragged the body fifty yards into the woodsy brush. She came back wiping her hands on her apron. She walked up to Edward and knelt in front of where he sat in the forest mulch.

"Edward, you have to remember that sometimes things have to be done, no matter how strange or distasteful they may seem at the time. Remember that." She stood and walked back to the cabin not looking to see if he followed her or not.

Edward sat there for a long time, more than an hour he guessed. Then he stood, wiped the tears from his eyes, and went back to the house.

That afternoon he thought about it again. Maybe his mother was right. Maybe some animals just didn't deserve to live. He wiped away the last of his tears. He had never killed anything not a mouse or a bird or even a rat. He wondered what it would feel like. Just to kill. He kept wondering.

Neither of them ever spoke of the dog again or what happened that summer afternoon at the lake when he was eight years old.

10

KING BRODERSON TAPPED his pen knife on the water glass in front of him and the ten people around the table in the meeting room at the Forest Glen City Library quieted.

"The regular meeting of the Forest Glen Barbershop Quartet Contest will come to order," King said. "I trust that all of you have read the six committee reports that were emailed to you. We're getting down to the nub here. Two more months and it will be show time."

"Seems like we're behind where we should be." The soft clear voice of Dr. Mildred Warnick contrasted sharply with King's booming baritone that begged for authority. "I mean we should have a lot more entries by now and we haven't had the good publicity that we had last year." Warnick was one of four doctors in town. She had a general practice. She was 38, single, slender, and attractive. King also thought she was a bit too self-contained and full of herself.

"Hey, we've had tons of good PR on the web," Ed Rathwood countered. "Our web site is getting hit all the time. We've had contact with all of the barbershop organizations in the country with good results. Usually we draw mostly from the West Coast, but we have had two entries from Denver."

"What's the latest entry figure, Grace?" King asked.

Grace Douglas, president of the University Women's Club, turned a leaf in her secretary's three ring binder. "As of the latest report this morning we have eighteen entries. That's four more than we had at this time last year. We're good."

"Fine, moving on. Rudy, you said there was some problem getting chairs? With the bleachers in the gym and the chairs the high school has, how many more do we need?"

"Last year we rented four hundred chairs from an outfit in Portland. We still had about two hundred people standing. If a fire marshal had visited us he would have closed us down. I'm suggesting we get six hundred chairs this year and allow no standees."

Rudy Gomez was a second generation Cuban. His parents had fled Cuban early on in the Castro regime and settled in Forest Glen. Rudy was a general contractor building small homes and other structures. He was a light chocolate color with black hair, stood five feet eight, and was in hard work great condition.

"Our budge will take this hit?" King asked looking at Jake Vining. The only CPA in town checked his notebook, flipped two pages, and nodded.

"Yep, unless you go wild on the stage and decorations." Jake was new to the barbershop committee this year as treasurer.

"Then with a voice vote the committee authorizes

you to get the added chairs. All in favor?" The chorus of 'ayes' sounded.

King went through the rest of his agenda. There were no problems with the tee shirt sale, the moustache contest, the welcoming group, or housing. Again this year most of the contestants would have to stay in motels in Hillsboro or Beaverton or hotels in Portland. Forest Glen had only two small hotels with a total of twenty four rooms.

King looked around at the group. Some of them hadn't said a word but that was fine with him.

"So, is there any new business to come before this committee?"

A small woman who insisted on wearing a hat whenever she left her home spoke up.

"What about this murder, Mr. Broderson. Will that have any ill effects on our contest? Will some peoples stay away because of the bad publicity we're having in the Portland papers and on TV?" Her name was Mrs. Maxwell Clark. She always used that name.

King looked over at Police Chief Sanderson

"I believe that there will be no long lasting problem," the chief said. "It will be a two day story in the paper and on TV. I have seen no national coverage of the story. We don't need to worry about this."

The widow Mrs. Maxwell Clark nodded at the Chief, touched a linen handkerchief to her brow, and put it away in her purse.

King closed down the meeting then glad that there were no big problems. This was his third and last year as chairman. Next year it would be somebody else's baby.

Ed Rathwood came up to the front and eyed King.

"You got the time for me to treat you to a piece of pie and some coffee? We need to talk."

Ten minutes later in the Forest Café, they worked on their pie and coffee. Ed put down his fork and let a small frown crawl over his face.

"King, maybe I'm getting cold feet about this shopping center. Our business has been in the same spot in the same building now for over sixty years. Dad opened up the place back in forty nine. People know where we are, feel comfortable coming in. A brand new store? Wow. I've started making some sketches and plans, but haven't seen an architect yet." He held up both hands as King started to say something.

"I know, King, I know. I gave you a verbal agreement that I'd take the spot right beside your store. How do you know that we'll get any traffic out there? Foot traffic isn't vital to a furniture store but it doesn't hurt. You signed up the anchor at the far end of the complex yet?"

"Fact is I have, Ed. A huge Home Depot is going in. Be about twice the size of my store and competitive in some areas, but be damn good for the center. A big draw. That help you change your mind?"

"Oh yeah. That's great. Big outfit. Heard about them. None in Hillsboro but I think Beaverton has one. Okay, I'm sold, again. I'll call an architect friend in Portland tomorrow."

King laughed. "Oh, yes. Great. Glad to know you're really on board. Now I can finish my pie.'

On his drive home, Ed had the strangest feeling, weird, like somebody was patting him on the shoulder. He couldn't help but look in the back seat. Nobody there. He knew that. He snorted. Hey, maybe his old man was patting him on the back. He snorted again. He'd never had any great belief in an afterlife. Religion and all it tried to foist off on people had always seemed to him to be a big lie. He shook his head. What a strange and unsettling feeling. He'd have to do some hard thinking about that.

11

CHIEF SANDERSON FELT a wave of relief knowing that Charlotte Alberts had at last been found. The town was exhausted. For three days they had scoured most of the town and much of the area around it. Two days they had over five hundred volunteers searching everywhere often for the second and third times.

Now the farmer had found her. The man was sure. He was friends with the family through the church. The Chief took only Young and Hardy with him on this first run. If it proved to be Charlotte, he would call in the Sheriff's men. A hundred questions rattled around in his head. Was this the same killer? Was it a chance happening? Did he have a serial killer on his hands? What would the news people do with this one?

Homer Long met them at a turnoff on the gravel road that led into his place and then six miles on up into the hills. No words were spoken. Long waved, pointed forward, and then drove down the duty road.

The Chief held back a hundred yards to let some of

the dust settle, but kept the Jeep in sight. They parked thirty yards from a falling in old three room house.

The four men crowded into the small room and looked down at the old mattress against the far wall. The girl lay there, fully dressed, her hair combed and arranged around her pale face. The dress was a pure white with blue birds embroidered on the shoulder and covered her chin to ankles. Gold slippers showed beneath the dress. Chief Sanderson compared the girl's face with a picture he carried.

"Yes, this is Charlotte Alberts, but those are not the clothes she wore when she was kidnapped." He went outside and used his cell phone. He was back in a few minutes.

"Sheriff and his team are on the way. Take them about a half hour to get here. Homer, will you lead them in when they get to your turnoff?

The farmer, rancher, and orchard man nodded.

Young and Hardy went outside, kept well back from the structure, but searched to see what they might find. Mostly they kicked out beer cans and fast food wrappers.

On a small grassy spot they saw a pair of blue panties and a blue tee shirt. They left them in place. Despite the Oregon summer rain, the ground was fairly had packed. No tire tracks showed that could be cast as evidence. They found where a car or light truck had backed up and turned around. At the farthest backing point a cluster of brush and small trees stopped the vehicle.

Hardy thought he saw something in the grass in front of the brush. He looked closer and near the bent back grass he saw part of a broken tail or stop light lens.

"Might be something," Hardy said. "If we can match it with some make and model."

"It will be a stolen car," Young said. "This killer wouldn't use his own wheels for a kill like this."

"Still it could lead somewhere." Hardy took a plastic evidence bag from his pocket and put the three inch square of red plastic inside. "Worth a try," he said.

It was over an hour before the sheriff's squad arrived with four cars, six officers, and the Medical Examiner. Hardy turned over his plastic lens part to the forensic men who were glad to get it.

Chief Sanderson called to his two men and got in the city cruiser and drove back to town.

Hardy was glad to get back and finish his day shift. Nothing else they could do at the crime scene. He had enough for a report. The county would have jurisdiction this time. He wondered if the killer was the same. There was no pattern. Nothing even similar. He thought of what had been bothering him. There had been no sign of blood in the cabin, or around the walk way inside. Was this another strangulation? That would be a match. But there were lots of ways to kill without leaving a blood trail. He'd work on that.

Hardy set up a new bulletin board area for Charlotte. He put down everything they knew about her from the three day search. He put it on his lap top, then printed it out in twenty-four point bold, and tacked it on the board.

Charlotte Anne Alberts
Age: thirteen
Junior in high school
Songsters, Booster's Club, Band, Straight A
Cut through the park going home from school

No boyfriend
Church Member, Youth Group
Second high schooler killed in a week

HARDY READ through the list again. Nothing there. No hint of a clue who kidnapped and killed her. Rape? Probably. Pedophile? Maybe. Why the new white dress, the combed hair, and even make up? He had no answers.

His phone rang.

"Jones."

"Hardy. Front desk. The Portland papers and TV are going to be calling. What should I tell them?"

"Only that Charlotte's body has been found in a shack in the hills west of Forest Glen. Cause of death not yet determined. The Chief of Police or the County Sheriff will have statements later."

Ten minutes after that the phone droned out a steady series of rings. Joanie at the front desk turned away the stream of reporters with her short statement.

Hardy got one call that sent him out on a fender bender crash near the university. It took him an hour to get the two parties talking and trading information. No one injured.

Young had two calls he responded to but for the most part it was a quiet day.

Hardy knew the Chief would be worried. He came out of his office looking like a cougar had used him for a scratching tree. He slammed his notebook down on Hardy's desk and flopped into his chair.

"Not a damn thing. The SO says no prints, no scrap of paper, so no evidence. Just a raped and murdered little girl who had her whole life out there waiting for her. Only mark on her body was a small wound over the heart. The ME said probably a thin knife that penetrated her heart and killed her instantly."

Chief Sanderson took off his hat and tossed it toward a chair. It missed. "Why the dress? The press is going to go bananas over this. Dressed up like a bride, they will say. Fresh new bra, new underwear, socks, and fancy slippers.

"The forensic guys went crazy. Not a damn thing besides that tail light lens piece you found. They rushed it down to Hillsboro where their auto expert pegged it to one of two makes. They checked the local dealerships and nailed the make, model, and year. A 2005 Honda minivan. Hillsboro had a stolen car report on such a rig. They found it in Cornelius half way between us and the county seat. Forensics guys are going over it now."

"So maybe something?" Hardy asked.

"Maybe. But this guy is so damn neat and clever that I don't have much hope."

"Sheriff's jurisdiction."

"Amen to that, but she's one of our kids."

"We don't know squat," Hardy said. He frowned. "They find her clothes?"

"Hey, nobody mentioned that. No clothes out there. Something we can work on here."

Hardy had never seen the Chief so down. He looked like he was ready to cry, scream, or throw a major fit.

"A TV truck from Portland charged in right behind the ambulance. Don't know how they found out about it. Be all over the news tonight."

The chief's phone rang twice. He swore softly, went into his office, and picked it up.

"Yeah, Sanderson here." He listened for a moment and a smile flooded his face. "No lie. That's for sure. At least we have something. Thanks. Call me with any more good news." He hung up.

"Be damned. Forensics found something on the stolen van. Looked like it had been wiped clean and vacuumed, they said. But in the carpet in the back they found some small granules. One of them thought it looked familiar and sure enough it's cat litter. The lady who owns the van does not have a cat. We can assume that the killer has a cat and some of the litter got kicked out and imbedded in his shoe soles. Then it fell out when he moved his victim around in the van. Maybe at last we have one damn clue to work with."

12

ED RATHWOOD SETTLED into the latest theater style seat, reached to his right, and pushed several buttons. A brilliant display of fireworks erupted on an eight by ten foot giant screen in front of him. As the best fireworks in the world exploded, Ed eased back in the chair.

He was in their home theatre, built years ago to hold twelve and refitted with new seats, a larger screen, and all of the electronic wizardry available a year ago.

His mother came into the half dark room pushing a small serving cart that she positioned between them then sat down in the second seat in the front row. The cart held a pair of already made drinks, plus the fixings for a dozen different concoctions.

"So we're fireworking tonight," Elmira Rathwood accused with a touch of whine in her voice. She eased into a more comfortable position and stared hard at her only child. "I thought we had the movie, 'The Psychotic Who Did Ellen."

"We do, the fireworks are to fill in the time until you

arrived. You realize we saw this flick about a month ago."

"I do, that's why I ordered it again. The hero is so flawed, yet at the same time so human that I love the beast."

Ed pushed more buttons and the fireworks snuffed out and some darkly brooding theme music flooded the room. The titles came on over the back of a man dressed all in black who was doing something to a woman on a couch. The knife he used dripped blood. The man turned and his head came full screen, eight feet high showing an agony twisted face smeared with blood. The man's eyes flickered with an inhuman orange glow then slowly fade into a deathly black.

The figure roared into a maniacal laugh and talked directly to the audience.

"You expected a fairy tale, a tender love story, or maybe an uplifting girl makes good? No such luck for you. You get me in all my gory glory. If someone gets cut and bleeds in this story, she really bleeds. If someone dies, he is dead forever more. So sit back and take a hard look at just how evil and monstrous a human being can be. Then I wish you pleasant dreams."

The picture shock cut to a scene with four young naked women of four ethnic types. Two were model thin and big breasted. One was chunky and the last one was over two hundred pounds fat. They were on a movie sound stage listening to a man dressed all in black.

"Ladies you will do exactly what I tell you to do. If I say undress, you undress. If I say put your clothes on you will do that. You are being paid well. As long as you follow orders you get paid. Fuck up and you'll be out on your ass so quick you won't have time to get dressed"

The speaker turned and we see he's the same one who did the introduction to the film. His face is more natural, but still dark and sullen. Before the girls can move, a naked man runs on the set with a sputtering, blue flame shooting butane torch. He chases the women off the set.

Forty five minutes later, Ed turned up the room's lights and punched off the movie.

"Intermission," Ed said. He was so bored he wanted to scream but his mother was here. It was a pact they had. Every Tuesday evening they watched a movie his mother selected. She liked anything that was dark, evil, demented, full of blood, murder, with ordinary people exploding out of their minds, and turning into ghoulish raging killers and ravishers.

"Mother, how do you know that James here is really psychopathic?"

His mother looked at him with a penetrating frown. "Edward, you know the signs and symptoms as well as I do. In this case our friend James has a series of hallucinations. First he thinks he's the man who shoots the steers in a slaughterhouse. He plays that out by mowing down six men in a neighborhood bar. Then he morphs into a butcher only he's working on naked women, not sides of beef. Surely you can see the symbolism the director is showing us."

"Yes, I see it. But James isn't out of his skull all the time. How can he be so normal most of the time and then get set off by something and go weird and crazy and murderous?"

"Edward. I thought we agreed that's what makes

the psychopath such an interesting character to study. One moment he's rational, the next second he's having delusions and playing them out in real time with real people. Marvelous." She drained her drink and held it up for Edward to refill. He did.

"Edward, I know you're forgetful sometimes, but surely I don't have to remind you about the thought disorder involved with the psychopath. Where he has an underlying disturbance of conscious thought. We saw it with James when he began speaking a hundred miles a second and couldn't write a complete sentence. James is a perfect example."

Ed mixed himself a fresh drink, sampled it, smiled, tried to listen to his mother's discourse on the criminally insane, and the random episodes of the true psychopath.

Ed started the movie again and didn't think it would ever end. He had seen this one so often he could talk through the dialog seconds before the actor on the screen did. He drifted off a moment and his mother spoke sharply.

"Enough turn it off. We never watch when James is captured. That ruins the whole aspect of our study. Turn it off, Edward."

13

HARDY JONES PUSHED the phone tighter to his ear as he listened to the County Crime lab man in Hillsboro talking about the cat litter from the stolen van.

"So we got a spectroscopic readout on the litter down to an eyelash. Six different chemicals. Now we have sent to the same lab in Portland five of the most popular cat litters sold so we can try to find a match."

"Five, huh," Hardy said. "That will be a big sample to try to trace the buyers. Could be hundreds of names."

"Not worried about that. The spec men said this sample they worked had a strange and unusual composition of chemicals."

"When do we get the results?"

"Guy said he was backed up but would do it in a day or two."

"Guess we'll just have to wait."

"Let you know soon as we get the word."

They talked a little more then hung up. Hardy looked at his desk. Two murders and they had almost nothing to go on. He checked the board with the list of facts about each case. From the sexual point of view it could well be two killers, one straight and one gay. He eyed the list on the first case. His glance stopped at the 20-year-old multi-painted car. He couldn't remember seeing any such rigs around town. There were the usual off-color car doors the owner had picked up from a junk yard.

That morning he checked two shops in town that did auto painting but neither of them remembered anything like the description of the killer's car.

"Jodie Barnes had an old Ford Fairlane he was reworking. He came in to talk to me twice about paint and what would work best. It already had about three coats he said."

"How old is the Fairlane?" Hardy asked.

"Fifteen, maybe eighteen years. And old one."

Hardy thanked him and found Jodie's address in the telephone book. His wife said Jodie was at work at the auto parts store. He'd be home about six.

"He still working on that Fairlane?" Hardy asked.

"Oh, yeah. I keep nagging him about all the money he spends on it. Keep it locked up in a work shed in back. I think he's afraid I might sell it to some auto wrecking yard."

Hardy made a note to come back about seven tonight and talk to Jodie. His cell phone sang its lonely tune and he answered. It was dispatch.

"Hardy, you had a call from county forensics. Guy sounded excited about something. Said for you to call him soonest."

"Will do. Thanks." Hardy punched the number he had put in his cell and a moment later the county crime lab answered. He asked about some new clue they had found.

"Oh, yeah. Big time. We went over that van again. One of our guys spotted a smudge on the inside top of the van. It's covered with a fabric and a dark stain a quarter of an inch showed."

"Blood?" Hardy asked.

"Damn right, some dried blood and three strands of short black hair. We think he banged his head when he carried the girl out, or maybe had a struggle with her. We're estimating he must be six one to six three to have that kind of a thump on his head."

"So we could have the killer's DNA?" Hardy asked.

"Unless something weird happens. The blood and the hair should give us perfect DNA."

"All we need is a match."

"My hunch is that he's new to the system. So we won't have a match in any of the DNA data banks here or in the state or nationally."

"Your estimated height might be a help, too."

"Hope so. We're looking at that mattress from the Charlotte kill, too. Never can tell."

Hardy ended the conversation and drove back to the station. He typed in the new clue on his lap top and printed it out so he could pin it on the display board. He did a quick report on the clue and left it on the Chief's desk.

Hardy stared at the board with the two killings on it. Something but nothing. No solid line of clues that could point at a suspect. It drove him nuts.

His desk phone rang. It was his wife.

"Well, we won six to three," she said.

"We won.....oh, damn. I promised the team that I'd

be there for the opener. We have two other coaches, were thy there?"

"One of them, Charlie."

"I'll be there for the Saturday game. These two killings are driving me crazy."

"I know, see you tonight?"

"I have a seven o'clock talk with a guy. Then I'll be home for sure. Got to go. Love you."

"Love you. Be careful out there."

Bob Young came whipping into the squad room a huge grin leading the way. He straddled a chair and laughed softly.

"Well our little Charlotte wasn't quite perfect after all. Turned out she did have a boyfriend ---sort of. He's fifteen and they met sometimes in the brushy part of the park after school. She may have been watching for him when she was snatched."

"The kid talked?"

"Yeah. He went to his minister and then they both talked to the Chief this afternoon at the church. The whole thing was innocent and platonic and an experimenting time. They held hands and that was about it. Lots of talking and laughing and making plans the kid said."

"Interesting, but another dry well," Hardy said. He told Bob about the blood, hair, and probable DNA evidence.

"Great," Young said. "Now all we need is a live body to match that DNA."

URIAH CONDIT HANDED Ed Rathwood the three orders he had worked out for replacement furniture and some new items. He did the preliminary work up then Ed went over them and added or deleted and sent out the orders.

"Thanks, Uriah. I'll get on these first thing in the morning."

"Good. Nothing urgent, but items we need. Oh, this is Thursday. Will you be needing any company for the weekend?"

Ed stared at Uriah for a moment then shook his head. "No, I don't think so. I'm actually feeling much calmer than I have in weeks. I thank you for your good work in the past, but nothing this time"

"Very good, Mr. Rathwood. I'll send the email notice and give them the message."

Uriah went down the stairs from his boss's second floor office. He had worked here for almost twenty five years. He in effect ran the place, taking care of the inventory, managing the other three members of the sales crew, and generally keeping the ship afloat. He also took care of Mr. Rathwood's more personal needs. But there was no appointment to make for the weekend.

The more he considered it, the more he thought that Mr. Rathwood had seemed more settled down, less nervous and sensitive lately. He wasn't sure just why but he would figure it out. Part of his job. Mr. Rathwood had been fair and more than generous with him over the years. He had worked for Edward's father for fifteen years and Edward had kept him on when the elder Mr. Rathwood died. He knew he was being paid at least fifty percent more than any other store manager in town. He smiled. He was worth it.

He settled in behind his small desk on the sales

floor in back and watched the displays. He had set them up in room patterns, so people could see how a particular piece would look with other furniture. These display changed weekly and it kept him busy working out new patterns.

He thought about Mr. Rathwood again. Yes, he had changed ever so slightly in the past week or so. He didn't seem to get tinges of depression the way he often did. He hadn't been to the river fishing for at least two weeks. It was what he did often when the pressures of the business overwhelmed him.

Why the past week or so? There had been no huge changes at the business. No big crises in Mr. Rathwood's home life that he knew of. No national crisis or stock market plunge.

Locally? There had been the two killings of young people. How could that affect Mr. Rathwood? No, too much of a stretch. He looked up, aware that he had been preoccupied, not paying attention to the floor.

The woman cleared her throat and he stood at once.

"Mrs. Bailey, I didn't notice you come in. Excuse my lack of attention. Can I show you that sofa and chair that you looked at last week?"

Upstairs, Ed watched the sales floor below. He had put his office where he could see most of the merchandise and the action. He smiled and leaned back in his chair. Yes, he had been right. He did feel more relaxed, and more in control than he had for months. The voices didn't come so often. The cold dark feelings didn't impose on him as much as they had even two weeks ago. Often he welcomed the voices. They helped him fight off the early pangs of depression. They told him that he was a success and he was doing fine. He was well off money wise. Some of his stocks and bonds had performed well despite the market shifts. He was considering retirement at the age of thirty five. Yes. He could fish all he wanted to. Go to Alaska for salmon and a dozen other species.

He turned on a TV set, found a sports channel, and watched a rerun of a football game. He blocked out the voices. He could do it easily today. They came at the strangest times. He wasn't ready. Not yet. For a moment he gloried in his fantastic performance a few days ago. Outstanding. He would relive that night again and again.

OFFICER HARDY JONES saw a five year old Honda parked in the driveway of Jodie's house and hoped that meant he was home. Jodie answered the door.

"Hey, I didn't do it. I was in California at the time." Jodie laughed. "So, what can I do for you, officer?"

"I'd like to take a look at your Fairlane. I hear you're restoring it."

"Yep. Costing a bundle but I'll get it all back and make a big profit when I sell it. How you know I have the Fairlane?"

"Paint shop guy told me."

They went around the house to what had once been a detached garage. Jodie unlocked it and snapped on the lights. Hardy's hopes smashed. The Fairlane was partly stripped. No wheels or axles and the whole body had been painted with an undercoat of dull brown.

"I figure I'm about half done. Worked the engine

and transmission first. All in top shape. Now I have the rest of it."

Hardy waved him off. "Thank, Jodie. This isn't the Fairlane that I'm looking for. Good luck with your project."

Back at the station, Hardy filed a quick report on the car paint try and the Fairlane then headed for home. He'd have a lot of explaining to do for missing the Little League team's first game.

14

KING BRODERSON KICKED a clod of dirt, watched the bulldozer dig into the soft ground, and push a load of soil ahead past a heavy wooden stake with a white flag on it.

"Why they going so deep?" King asked.

Ed Rathwood pointed. "Down about ten feet now that should be it. You've got to have a solid foundation down there for a two story building. Don't worry they know what they're doing."

"If they don't I'm wasting two point eight million dollars."

"In five years this King Shopping Center will be worth ten times that. Glad you're getting it started."

"About time. The judge threw out that damn law suit about the traffic and the schools."

"Full speed ahead. You have a completion date?"

"Had but we got held up."

"I talked to an architect in Portland. He's coming up with some plans for my new store. Damn but it looks huge compared to what I have now."

"I kept telling you that you were too crowded there. This will give you a chance to expand your lines and get new ones. Maybe some big brand names."

"Hey, man, don't scare me any more than I already am. I'm half paralyzed the way it is."

"You'll get over it. Look at that guy shove that dirt around. That pile is going to be twenty feet high before long."

They walked down to where the King Supermarket would end and Ed's place would begin.

"Right here?" Ed asked.

"Exactly. We're neighbors. Home Depot is set to begin construction next week down on the far end. They will throw a lot of people on it and probably be done before my place is finished."

"Okay, we've walked it. Let's get out of here and find that cup of coffee and Danish you offered me," Ed said.

They went back downtown and had coffee at the Glen Café with sides of Danish.

"I can't believe it," King said "A buck forty nine for a cup of coffee."

"Believe it. Or just take a look at the prices in your store. Food costs are going out of sight."

"Anything new on the barbershop contest?" King asked.

"You're the big cheese on that one. You will know if anything fouls up. So far looks smooth and on schedule."

They had seconds on coffee. King said he always felt better with a refill. That cut the cost of a cup of coffee in half.

Ten minutes later they both headed for their stores and the rest of the morning.

AT THE POLICE STATION, Hardy had another email from the county lab. They had reports back on two of the kitty litter samples and no matches with the litter from the van. "Three more to go," the email said.

Hardy showed the email to the chief who slammed it down on his desk. "Get the rest of the troops in here. We're in trouble. Get everyone."

Hardy and Bob Long were in the squad room. He called the other two patrolmen. Doug Olson had just got home from his night shift and swore for a solid minute, then said he'd be there in half an hour. Patrolman Al Turley wasn't home and he didn't answer his cell phone. He was a bachelor and it was hard telling where he might be. The Chief glared at Hardy then nodded.

"Okay, troops. We're in deep shit here. It's been ten days since Willy died and we don't have squat. Yeah, something about an old car and a thirty two year old guy. Oh, yeah, that damn cat litter. That's no place. The mayor and the city council are still in shock, but they read the old riot act to me. Move on it now or they'll turn it over to the sheriff."

He dropped into his chair

"We've got that DNA coming," Hardy said.

"That's a County case. Anyway we're not sure that the Charlotte kill is by the same person as Willy. I won't let this one go cold. We've got to develop something. Go back over all our contacts, dig, and dig again, and see what you can find. We've got to get a lead or clues of some kind."

"I still think that the teacher is involved," Hardy said. "I'm checking her out tonight."

"Keep it on the quiet and safe side," the Chief said.

"I'll go back to the frat house and prowl around," Young said. "Somebody there might know more than he's saying."

"Has the county looked into that dress that Charlotte was wearing?" Officer Olson asked. "If it was purchased locally..."

"Yeah, get on that today. Now, what else?" He looked around at the unresponsive men. "Okay, I know how you feel. But if we don't turn up something damn soon, the papers, and TV are going to be calling us a bunch of hicks in the sticks. Now get out of here and bring me some good news."

It was before noon that Hardy went to the high school and had them pull the girl out of class who he had talked to before. She didn't know why she was called out but nodded when she saw Hardy.

"Hey, Officer Jones. Can you fix a traffic ticket for me? It wasn't my fault."

Hardy chuckled. "I've heard that one over a hundred times. I need to know if you've thought of anything else about the car or the man who picked up Willy after school that day."

She sobered. "I was kidding about the ticket. I don't even drive yet. The car. Wow. It was old, about five or six colors of paint, rattled a lot, but the engine sounded good as it went past me. About the man. Wow again. I'd say he was Caucasian, not black or Latino. Maybe a little sun tanned. I just got a quick look."

"You said the car went past you and then slowed and stopped just past Willy. So he had to walk up to the passenger's side?"

"Right. That's what I saw. Seemed like they talked a little, then Willy opened the door, got in, and the car drove on down the street."

"Did it turn off School Lane?"

"Could have. Lots of streets lead off it. I didn't watch it anymore after it left."

"Anything else?"

"About Willy. I know it was him. That little hitch and swagger when he walks. And he had on a letterman's jacket. You know the kind the guys get when they earn a spot on a sports team."

Hardy made some notes then looked up at the pretty girl. "Hey, gonna be all over school that you got busted this morning. You can tell them that actually you're working undercover for the DEA on a big drug bust."

She laughed. "I just might do that. But now my cover is broken, right?" She giggled and hurried out the door of the empty classroom.

Hardy took a deep breath. Not a damn thing new. Maybe the letterman's jacket. There must be a hundred of them around the school. He'd put it in his report.

Hardy gave a print out on his talk with the girl, and then added a note on the bulletin board in twenty four point bold: "Letterman's jacket and other clothes Willy wore that last day are all missing."

IN THE AFTERNOON Hardy had one call to a crash out by cemetery hill. Two injured and the ambulance came and two tow trucks. It was after four when he got back to the station.

He finished a quick report, printed it out and filed it, then headed for the teacher's apartment. He hoped that Madelyn Tesser came home, got dressed up wild, and went to some place unlawful. The sexy, big-busted high school teacher may or may not have had sex with the dead football star. Somehow she didn't respond the right way when they questioned her. He had her address and knew she usually came home to her apartment about four-thirty. He had changed into civilian clothes and drove his own car. She lived in one of the better apartment houses in town. He parked where he could see the entrance to the parking lot and scrunched down in the seat waiting. He'd been on what seemed like hundreds of stake outs, but this one could be more interesting. He was armed with a 48-ounce Coke and a dozen cookies his wife had made yesterday.

It was a slow night. By eleven o'clock the Coke was gone and he only had two cookies left. He had seen Miss Tesser arrive home about four-thirty, park, and then go in the center entrance. She drove a two-year-old Chevy SUV. That was the last he saw of her. Her car never moved. He gave up at midnight and went home.

Cindy had curled up on the sofa and not even a horror movie on TV had kept her awake. She came upright at once when he closed the back door.

"Anything?" she asked.

"No, and your cookies saved the night. News time or did I miss it?"

"Missed all the way around."

"Miss Tesser gets one more stake out tomorrow night, then I'll have to give up on her. I still think she lied through her moustache when we interviewed her. The problem is we can't prove it, and even if we could, we don't know if she had anything to do with Will's murder."

Cindy grinned. "Come on, big cop guy. I think it's time you stop fantasizing about that woman and let me show you a new little trick about making love."

"New? What can be new?"

She showed him.

15

FRIDAY MORNING the Forest Glen Police had a visitor. He was Lieutenant Johnson of the Washington County Sheriff's Office and was in charge of the Charlotte murder. He had been talking with Hardy and Bob Young for an hour about the case.

"We're nowhere on this one," Johnson said. "Not a hint of a clue about any suspect. That kitty litter may be our one hope, but that's slim to sad. We're not even sure the killer was a man, although the rape seems to indicate that."

"So do we have one killer here or two?" Hardy asked.

"Could be this thirty-something guy your witness saw or a six-footer who banged his head in the van. One could be straight and the other one queer." Johnson laughed. "Yeah, I know, not supposed to call them fags or queers anymore. Long time habit is hard to break. You think one or two killers?"

"No evidence, just a gut feeling that it's the same guy," Hardy said. "He's smart, clever, wears gloves, and must plan out each kill with the patience of a bird watcher. I bet he tracked Charlotte several days before he decided where to hit her."

Johnson closed his lap top and stood. "In some ways I agree. At least now you know all we have on this one, and we're up to date on that first kill. Let's plan on meeting once a week to keep in touch."

ACROSS TOWN and up the slope of the hills on Fir Lane just inside the city limits, Rudy Gomez checked progress on the current house he had contracted to build. It was more than half done. The framing was up, the roof and sidewalls on and most of the rooms inside framed and dry walled. The plumbing and electrical had been inspected and signed off on last week.

He was proud of his work. This was the most expensive home he had built so far. He had been a contractor now for five years, and had moved up from home repairs to remodeling, to building new homes from scratch with a contract. Most people called him Rudy. He had fit in to the small town quickly and was accepted as a solid citizen.

He was a Cuban he told everyone who asked. His parents had fled Cuba shortly after Castro had taken over. He had worked hard at becoming an American and had won his citizenship.

Several of his workers were Mexican, and he was careful to hire only legal ones or with a green card. He was not a union shop but had quality finish carpenters and workers to do a fantastic job. The finished house would sell on the market for well over a half million dollars. He had contracted to do the work for

$375,000 and figured that he should clear at least $80,000.

He went downstairs, outside, and looked at the exterior. The dual pane windows were all in, the doors on, and the siding would be on by next week. He should finish the work two weeks ahead of his projected end date.

Rudy served as his own foreman. He was a master carpenter and knew the home building inside out. He watched two of his men working on the flooring in the living room, then headed for Miller's Hardware for some special light bulbs he would need for the track lighting in the den.

He drove his ninety-four Ford pickup that showed the battle scars of many construction projects.

Rudy didn't notice the black Toyota that followed him from half a block back. When Rudy went into the hardware store, the black Toyota cruised past then continued up the street.

HARDY WORKED the rest of the day trying to figure out some new angles or new ideas about the two murders. He came up empty. In the afternoon he had two traffic calls for fender benders and settled in at his watch spot at four o'clock to see what his favorite high school teacher would do today.

She drove in a little after four thirty. Hardy took out a thermos of coffee and a sandwich Cindy had made for him that morning. He was out of cookies but had a backup Big Gulp 48-ounce Pepsi for later on.

At seven o'clock her car started and left the complex parking lot. Hardy followed her a half block back. She drove to the west, went up a hill and into a row of five new homes that were better than most in town. She parked and went up to 334 Forest Lane and rang the bell. A moment later she went inside. Hardy parked two houses down where he had a good view of the front door and waited.

Within five minutes three more solo women arrived in cars and went inside the same house. It was still light enough that he recognized one of the women, Dr. Mildred Warnick, one of the town's four doctors and the only female. The other two women looked to be in their late thirties and all were dressed well but not flashy.

A woman's meeting? What kind? Hardy wondered. Maybe an investment club. Were those still popular? It could be a book club where they all read the same book, then got together and talked about it. It could be anything: a tea party, a social club, a computer club, or even a bridge game.

Another woman came about seven thirty. She was dressed all in black and didn't bother to knock, just opened the door and walked in.

After that nothing for two hours.

He had long finished the sandwich and the coffee. He started on the Pepsi that still had some ice left. From where he watched he could see the near side of the target house. Movement caught his eye and he concentrated on the shadows. Someone came up the side of the house probably from the alley. It had to be a man and over six feet tall. The figure tried the side door, opened it, and vanished inside.

What in hell? Was he going to rob the women? For a second Hardy thought of charging the house and warning the women, but he didn't. The man acted like he knew the door would be unlocked. So why was he there?

At a quarter to ten the women began to leave. He saw only four come out. Five had gone inside.

A half hour later Hardy saw the same side door open and a tall figure come out. He hesitated then walked to the front of the house and down the sidewalk toward town.

Hardy followed him well back. The man went a block then cut over a block then unlocked a beat up Ford. Before he could start the car, Hardy pulled his car in front at an angle blocking him off. Hardy jumped out of his car and ran up to the Ford's driver window. It was down.

"Police. Keep your hands on the wheel where I can see them."

"What the hell? What is this?"

"That's what I want to know. I'd like to see your driver's license."

Hardy saw that the man was young, maybe twenty. He growled as he pulled out his license. Hardy looked at it briefly in the beam of the small flashlight he always carried.

"So, Vance, what have you been doing tonight?"

"Coming back to the frat house from talking with my girl. A law against that?"

"So why did you park two blocks from her house?"

"Her dad doesn't like me."

"What about the six women in the house back there? Did they like you?"

"What? I was seeing my girl, Jenny."

"Then let's go back there to 304 Forest Lane and talk with your girlfriend."

"She's in bed by now."

"What about the six women in the hose, Vance? I saw them go inside. I saw you go in a couple of hours later by the side door. Now what's going on?"

Vance seemed to shrink into the car seat. "Oh, shit. I told them it was too risky. They said whatever goes on behind closed doors in a private house is nobody's business."

"They are on cocaine?"

"Maybe one or two. Look I didn't do anything illegal."

"You have a snort?"

"Just one. They insisted."

"What did they do for three hours?"

"Oh, thought you knew. It's a bridge club. They play a crazy kind of bridge. I couldn't understand it. Look, I'm kind of worn out. I'd like to get back to the frat house."

"Not quite yet. How often do they meet?"

"Every Friday night. This is the third contest."

"Contest? For a winner. The big winner at bridge gets a prize?"

"Yeah. Can I go now?"

"Not quite yet. What was the prize?" Hardy had figured it out. He wanted the kid to admit it.

"What was the prize, Vance? Was it you all naked and hot in a bedroom waiting for the prize winner?"

"Yes. Still nothing illegal. Consensual sex."

"And after the sex you get a reward of some kind. What was it, Vance?"

"Just a little reward."

"More specific, Vance. Two hundred dollars?"

"No it was a hundred and eighty. There was a thirty dollar entry fee."

"Now we're talking illegal. Male prostitution. I could run you in right now and then get those six women as the Janes who solicited."

"Oh shit. I'll be kicked out of school and my Dad will kill me."

"Maybe not. Get out of the car, I want to take a few pictures of you, close ups. Then you get back to your house and tell the brothers that the bridge game is over. We may bust them for drugs. You may get off free. I'll talk with the Chief about you. Vance Sawyer. I'll keep that name on record."

Hardy took four pictures of Vance with his digital camera that he always carried.

"Okay big stud, you're free to go. Be sure to stop at every stop sign you see. Oh, just curious. Who was the lucky bridge game winner?"

"Oh, God, you should have seen her. She's a teacher at the high school. Nobody used names. Biggest damn tits I've ever seen."

"Good bye Vance Sawyer."

THE NEXT MORNING Hardy printed out the digital shots on five by seven photo paper, then went in to talk to Chief Sanderson."

"That's the gist of it, Chief. I could nail the kid for prostitution and the six women as solicitors."

The Chief shook his head. "Not a chance. Not worth it. We don't need a big scandal right now or say that Doc Warnick was one of them, and Miss Tesser another? Kind of figures."

"Maybe we could throw a scare into tem. How about a drug raid? The kid said they were snorting cocaine. Probably some pot around too."

The Chief tapped his pen on a pad. "Get in touch with Vance. Tell him not to tell anyone at the frat that the place got busted. Let them set it up for next Friday. Then half way into the party we bust the place for coke and pot."

"We can scare hell out of them," Hardy said. "We hit the hunk too if he's there."

"Which doesn't help us at all on our two murder cases. Anything more on that cat litter?"

"I hope so. I'll call the crime lab right now for a double check."

16

ED SAT at his desk staring down at the sales floor below. He felt light headed. For just a second or two he realized what that meant and then he was gone.

He was in New York City in his 42nd floor luxury apartment overlooking Central Park. Two of his girls had been giving him trouble. One wanted out. Another one wanted to go back to art school. He had talked to both of them. Where else could they make the kind of money they made working with him? Nowhere.

He had six of the top call girls on the market and he charged from one to four thousand dollar a night for them. Most worked five or six night a week. They each had their own upscale apartment and made half of the nightly fee. Most had fifty or sixty thousand dollars in the bank.

Cecelia was the main problem. She turned down two customers lately because they were too rough. Yesterday she had said she was through. If he gave her any trouble, she would go to the vice squad, ruin him, and put him in prison for five to ten.

He set up a meeting with her in her digs for this afternoon. He arrived a half hour early, used his key, and made certain preparations. Cecelia arrived five minutes before the appointed time. She had been shopping. As usual, he thought.

"I wasn't sure that you'd come," he said.

"Why not? I told you I was through. I'm not afraid of you in spite of your threats."

"Tremendously brave of you, Cecelia." He stepped closer to her, grabbed her by the hair, and swung her onto the nearby couch. He followed up quickly before she could move. His knife came out and he plunged it deeply into her heart. Blood seeped out around the six-inch knife blade. Cecelia's eyes widened, then went blank, she shuddered once, and then let out a long last breath.

He held the knife in place until he was sure that she was dead. If he pulled the blade out, the blood would surge for a minute or so. Clean up would be a problem.

He shrugged. Why clean up at all. Leave her here. He quickly went through her purse and a small desk, removing his phone number from two places and a photo from an album. Satisfied, he went to the door and eased it open. He looked both ways along the hallway. No one there. He stepped into the hallway and walked down to the stairs. Two floors down, he went back to the hallway and the elevator. There would be no one who could identify him.

Ed stirred at his desk and shook his head. New York, what in the world? He stared at his desk. Was it a day dream or something more serious? He had read about hallucinations. Probably. They didn't hurt a thing, just took up time. He checked his watch. He had only ten minutes to meet the architect with the final plans to go to the county. He shivered for a moment. He was still a little queasy about the whole move. Too damn late now he was committed. He headed for the door and his meeting in the Glen Motel was the man had spent the night.

HARDY JONES GAVE a yelp of delight and red the email again:

"Jones. We have a match. This is one of the most expensive brands that we tested. Can you check stores in Forest Glen to see if they handle this brand? They call it PussyFoot."

Hardy left a note for the Chief, and then toured four grocery stores, two drug stores, and a pet store that all sold kitty litter. Management said they didn't stock PussyFoot. It was too expensive. He went to the combination pet store and vet and asked about the litter. The manager grinned and said they sure did have it in stock.

"I think you'll like it. It cost about twice what the cheap brands do but masks the odor for three or four times as long."

"This is a police matter not personal. Do you know who you sell this brand to?"

"Absolutely. All of our sales are in the computer with the customer's membership card number."

"I'd like a list of the customers who have bought PussyFoot during the past six months."

"We don't share our customer's..."

Hardy waved to silence him. "Are you the owner?"

"Oh, no. That would be Dr. Hendricks."

"Is he in? I need to see him at once."

"I could get you an appointment..."

"No. This is a police matter. I need to see him right now."

"Oh, sounds serious. I'll go see if he can come and see you. He may be with a patient."

Two minutes later a small man in a doctor's white coat came out of a side door. When he saw Hardy in uniform he sobered.

"Yes, officer. How may I help you?"

Hardy explained.

"This case has to do with a criminal act?"

"It does a serious one."

"Then we'd be glad to generate a list for you. Our computer can single out the customers for you. Shouldn't take more than about five minutes."

A short time later a pert little dark eyed girl in hospital scrubs came out with the printout. Hardy yelped in pleasure. There were twelve names on the page. He thanked the girl and hurried out to his patrol car. He took a quick rundown of the names. He recognized two of them, including Dr. Warnick and Rudy Gomez, the contractor.

Hardy called the station on the car's radio.

"Joanie. Tell the Chief that I found the retailer of the litter and I have twelve names of customers. Some of them he knows. Be back there soonest."

Minutes later Chief Sanderson looked over the list. He scowled. "Three women on the list, which we can discount. Leaves us nine men."

"How do you want me to pursue these guys?"

"We have a small bit of evidence here. But even if we knew for sure the killer, this kitty litter would not be enough even to get a search warrant. We'll work these men one at a time. It's pretty slim. A good defense lawyer could get us laughed out of court if that's all we have. We need some hard evidence. An eye witness would be good."

"We still setting up that drug raid on that sex house?"

"Yes. Let's just scare the hell out of all six of them. Be good for them. Young do any good at that frat house?"

"Haven't heard from him."

Hardy looked back at the list. "Most of these guys must work. I'll try to catch them about dinner time. First one on the list of cat owners is Quint Ingles. There's my phone." It was Joanie. She sent him on a domestic dispute call down by Carnation Lumber Mill. Not the best part of town. Hardy got in his patrol car and made the run. These calls were some of the most dangerous to go on. You never could tell what might show up and who might have a weapon.

RUDY GOMEZ PARKED his pickup outside the Taco Bell and got out. He pretended to be adjusting his outside mirror. He was watching a black Toyota that he thought had followed him all the way from the job site. He couldn't be sure. It had parked half a block away, but no one left the rig. Rudy frowned. He thought he saw the same SUV yesterday near his job. He shrugged. Probably just a coincidence. He went into the café and moved to the far window where he could see the same black Toyota. It hadn't moved. He could see no one inside. He patted one of the large pockets on his white carpenter's coveralls. Down in the right hand pocket he carried a small six shot .22 caliber pistol. He didn't have a permit for it, but he thought he needed it. It made him feel a lot safer.

He ordered a special burrito, a Pepsi, and settled down at one of the tables to eat. When he looked down the street, the black Toyota SUV had left the parking spot. Rudy shrugged. It was the best burrito he'd eaten all week.

17

ED FOUGHT it as long as he could. He had come awake that morning drenched in a sweat soaked sheet. He took a long shower, showed up late at the store, and took off at ten o'clock to go fishing.

But the Wilson River, thirty miles west of Forest Glen in the Coast Range, didn't settle him down the way it did some times. He caught two trout, released them, and then bellowed out a scream of fury, despair, and agony.

He sat on the bank of the Wilson, tears streaming down his face. He had never thought that he would become depressed. But a dark cloud of evil smelling mist blanketed him and made him scream again. Someone fishing downstream looked up, stared for a minute, and then went back to fishing.

Slowly Ed beat back the black fog and gradually he stemmed the tears. Finally he wiped away the last of the wetness and nodded. It was plain what he had to do. He had planned on another week of observation on the chosen one but now there wasn't time. The more he set up the plan the calmer he became. It would have to be tonight. The chosen one did not have any civic duty meeting tonight. He would be at home. The ruse to get him to the selected spot would have to work. He had planned it out well and figured it would do the job.

He gathered up his fishing tackle and walked back to the car. As soon as he came to the vehicle he saw the scratch from bumper to bumper half way up the side panels of the car. Someone with a key had left a message. It was the third time he had been scratched this way. The dealership had some magic paste they bluffed into the scratch and made it almost invisible. He forgot about it as he drove back home. Yes, a quick shower, then check in at the store and sign the payroll checks. Uriah would have them ready.

Ed wondered how much Uriah knew. He was sharp. Maybe too sharp for his own good. No, he might speculate but that would be all. He knew about the weekend visits. His boss's mood swings were one thing but Uriah trying them to anything else would be pure guess work. He paid Uriah too much for him even to think about that kind of guessing.

IT WAS JUST a minute after ten that evening when Ed made the call from a phone booth near the library. It was one of the few public use phones left in town. Cell phones had killed the phone booth.

"Yes, this is Rudy."

"Hey, just saw some kids tearing into that new house you're building out west of town. They had a pickup and looked like they would steal anything not nailed down."

"Hey, thanks. I'll charge right out there." Rudy hung up. Ed grinned.

Ed had parked a black Chevy pickup a block from the half built house on Fir Lane and waited. He had been a mile closer to the target than Rudy and beat him there. He changed his mind and drove up to the house and parked in front. He hurried inside the front door opening that hadn't had the door hung yet. Just inside he leaned against the wall and took out a small bottle, a big cloth, and waited.

Rudy had been on Ed's list for some time. He hated over achievers. The star football player. He would have been a big name at State then a pro. The little girl who was a straight A student and involved in all the extra activities. He just couldn't stand perfection. He didn't get to attain his dream of becoming a doctor. Why should others be able to live their dream? It was so unfair. He tried to even the scales just a little.

Rudy was only five seven. He wouldn't have any trouble with him. Ed soaked the big handkerchief again with chloroform from a small bottle. A moment later Rudy arrived skidding his work pickup to a stop in the dirt front yard in a cloud of dust. He jumped out and charged the front door. He held something in his right hand but Ed couldn't see what.

Rudy stormed inside the front door opening and stopped. Ed jumped him from behind, wrapped his right arm around Rudy's neck in a strangle hold, and pushed the chloroform soaked cloth against his nose and mouth.

Rudy struggled. His arms flailed.

A gunshot blasted into the closed room and Ed felt the shock of a bullet smashing into his thigh. Before Rudy could pull the trigger again he passed out from the soaked rag and slumped in Ed's arms.

Something hit the floor with a clatter and Ed figured it was the gun. His leg hurt like a crocodile had chomped on it. Blood. He couldn't leave any blood here. He dropped Rudy to the floor and felt of his right thigh. His pants leg was getting damp. He took a roll of tape out of his backpack and wrapped it tightly around his thigh, binding the pants leg to his leg. Then he took a spare shirt from his back pack and wrapped it around his leg and taped it fast. That should soak up all of the blood. He had no idea how deep the bullet went.

Now to find the gun. He took out a flashlight from his pocket and shone it around the floor. He found the small weapon quickly, an automatic, maybe a .32 or a .22. He pocketed it and turned back to Rudy. He held the small flashlight in his mouth as he picked up the contractor and headed for the stairs to the second floor.

He had hoisted Rudy over his shoulder and carried him upstairs. Ed found the third bedroom had not yet had the ceiling finished. He put Rudy on the dusty floor and tied his hands with plastic riot cuffs like the ones the police use.

Then he took out two lanterns from his back pack with the big square batteries and turned them on. He looked at his leg. The bullet must not have gone deep. No blood showed on his shirt around his thigh. Maybe the only plowed a furrow down the side of his thigh. His leg hurt like fire. It would need some medical attention. He would dispose of the little gun later where no one would find it.

He took off the backpack and arranged his tools of death on the floor. He put a gag around Rudy's mouth in case he came to then began a search of the first floor. He found what he wanted after ten minutes, a nail gun with 16 penny nails loaded in it.

He brought up a two foot high work stool and placed it under one of the ceiling rafters. He tossed a no stretch nylon rope over the two by six and knotted one end around it, then let the rest of the rope hang down.

Rudy had come around, writhed on the floor, and growled through the gag.

"Don't worry, Rudy, this won't take long. Have to stand you up now. Hope you don't mind. Can you help me get you upright?"

Rudy bleated in fury.

"Guess not. I'll use the old bottle of juice on you again. Amazing how quick that stuff works." He soaked the tail of Rudy's shirt with the chloroform and pushed it against Rudy's nose and mouth. Moments later he was unconscious. Ed dropped the empty bottle but didn't see where it went.

It took Ed ten minutes to tie a noose in the rope and then get Rudy up on the two foot high stool. He pulled the nose over Rudy's head and around his neck. Rudy stood on the stool, the noose holding him upright but doing no damage.

Ed sat down a moment puffing from the work. He wasn't in that good of shape after all. Ed started at Rudy. Tough luck, man, he thought, then kicked the stool from under Rudy's feet.

His body dropped a foot and the rope tightened around Rudy's throat. It wasn't enough of a drop to break his neck but the rope would strangle him slowly.

Ed cut the plastic cuffs off Rudy's hands and feet, putting the plastic in his backpack. Rudy was still unconscious from the chloroform or the rope. Ed took off the gag and put it in his backpack.

He picked up the nail gun and shot one of the four inch box nails into Rudy's thigh. Then he moved the gun up to Rudy's heart and fired six nails into his heart area. Any one of them could have killed Rudy. Ed felt the tension and the screaming nerves fading. He watched Rudy more and the black mists that had been lingering vanished. Ed took a deep breath. It was almost over.

Ed kept shooting the nails into Rudy's chest, neck and torso until it ran dry.

Yes, the numbing tensions were gone, the black thoughts and the desperate feeling of worthlessness. All gone. He wanted to shout celebrating his victory.

Instead he put the nail gun in his back pack, left the up ended stool where it was and picked up everything that he had brought with him.

He paused at the door, went back, and searched Rudy's front pants pockets until he found the keys to the builder's pickup. He checked the latex gloves he wore. Neither one showed rips nor tears.

Downstairs he thought about the gun Rudy had used. It was in his backpack. He had been lucky. If Rudy had lifted the gun anther few inches, Ed knew he would be dead. He went out to check the stolen black pickup. He had left nothing inside and had worn gloves when he drove here. He went to Rudy's pickup, got in, and drove away.

A few minutes later he parked two blocks from Dr. Warnick's apartment. Lights were still on. He went to the side door and knocked. He had to knock twice before he saw a light come on in the kitchen and a voice wavered through the outside door.

"Yes, who is it?"

"Ed Rathwood. I need some help."

She opened the door, saw Ed, and let him inside.

"Now what help?"

Ed showed her the bloody wrappings around his right thigh.

"Yes, you need some help." She sat him down in a kitchen chair and took off the bloody cloth and his pants.

"Milly, we have some secrets, you and I. Have I ever told anyone about our various little games and contests?"

"Not that I know of. Ed. I can tell when I see a bullet wound. Is anyone going to go to the police about this?"

"No. No one. This has to be our biggest secret. Do I have your word?"

"You do, Ed. But you owe me one huge favor. I mean gigantic. I'll think of something."

"Can you patch me up?"

"Like new. Not deep. The bullet went in and came out. Some cleaning out, and disinfecting and then some stitching. Have you ever had any stitches?"

"No."

"Okay. They will hurt, but not that much. Just relax

and try to think of something else. Like the last time you had a really good fuck."

"That was with you."

"Why thank you, Ed. I'm sure you don't mean it, but nice to tell me. Now relax. I've got some work to do here."

It took twenty two stitches and one stiff shot of whiskey for Ed before she was done. Then she bandaged it and told him to see her in three days.

"No appointment, just drop in and say it's about the barbershop."

He thanked her, kissed her lips, and limped the two blocks to Rudy's pickup. He left it parked downtown then walked a mile to his big house at the edge of the village.

The minute he stepped into the house his mother pounced on him.

"Ed, were in hell have you been? I've been trying to get your cell phone since eight o'clock. Your mangy old cat is sicker than a dog."

Ed stared at her. He was on such an emotional high that he barely heard what she said. Oh, yeah, his cat was sick.

"So, Mother. Why didn't you just kill it the way you did my other cat? You hate cats. Right now I can't be bothered. Go on kill the feline and get rid of her. I'm going to have a stiff drink and celebrate. Don't bother me. I'll be up in my den over the garage." He turned and left the room.

His mother watched him go, a strange smile touching her face for a moment. She nodded to herself and went to dispose of the cat. That was her boy, all right. He had that look she didn't see often on his handsome face. He had just done something, or he would soon do something strange or bizarre. He said he was going to celebrate. Maybe some deed was already done. She knew his look she just wasn't sure what it meant. That was the first time she realized that Edward was not psychotic. He was far, far beyond that. She would have to watch him closely for the next few days and see how he acted and watch for any strange behavior.

18

HARDY JONES WAS the first officer on the scene. A dry wall man had called the police station when he came to work at the Fir Lane address where Rudy Gomez was building a new house. Hardy arrived at eight oh four after dispatch had alerted him.

Hardy shook his head as he stared at Rudy were he hung from the rafter. He had been dead for some time. Hardy could see the nails sticking out of his chest as well.

"I didn't touch nothing," Pedro Sanchez, the dry wall man, said. "I watch those cop shows on TV."

"Good, thanks Pedro. You found him here at fifteen minutes to eight this morning?"

"Yes sir. First thing I called the police."

"Thanks, Pedro. You can go back to work now or whatever you think proper. We've a job to do here."

Pedro left and Hardy called dispatch confirming the dead body and asking Joanie to notify the sheriff. She had already called Chief Sanderson. Hardy checked Rudy's feet a foot off the floor and saw the tipped over stool he must have stood on. The rope would have cut off his air and strangled him in short order. Who would want to kill Rudy Gomez?

Chief Sanderson had the same question when he puffed up the stairs a few minutes later.

"Why the hell Rudy? Everyone liked him. He built good houses."

Hardy had been looking at the floor. It was sifted with the dry wall white powder. He found where Rudy must have been put on the floor. Another spot could have been a box or a back- pack. He found spots that where the dust was imprinted with two four inch squares.

"The killer must have struck last night," Chief Sanderson said. "I called his wife on my way here. She's worried. Rudy didn't come home last night. He got a phone call late and went tearing out of the house without saying where he was going."

"Look at these mark in the floor dust," Hardy said. "Seem to be the same size as those big batteries some small lanterns use. He had to have some light in here."

"Joanie said she'd notify the county," the Chief said. "They'll get a medical examiner and the forensic guys over here." The Chief stared at the scene his arms akimbo.

"Is that Rudy's pickup out front?" the Chief asked.

"I'll check it," Hardy said and headed down the stairs. In the glove box he found registration and insurance cards for Homer Davis, with a Hillsboro address. A stolen rig the killer used? If so where was the pickup Rudy always drove?

Hardy used his cell and asked Joanie to check with county sheriff and see if they had a stolen car report on a two thousand two Chevy half ton pickup. She said she'd get back to him on his cell.

Back upstairs, Hardy told the Chief about the truck which might be stolen.

The chief scowled. "Say Rudy left his house in a rush. He must have driven over here. He parks in front and charges inside and gets hung. So where is his pickup?"

"And how did the killer get away?" Hardy asked. "He could have switched pickups and driven Rudy's back to town."

The chief used his cell. "Joanie put Long, Olson, and Turley all on duty today. Have them search for Rudy Gomez's pickup. Get the license from DMV."

"So now we wait for the forensic guys." Hardy said.

Chief Sanderson shook his head. "I still can't figure why anyone would want to kill Rudy Gomez."

BY THE TIME the county officers arrived, Chief Sanderson had found a small bottle in a corner of the room. It was covered with the drywall dust. The Chief took a sniff at the opening and jolted backward.

"Whoa. That's chloroform. Might be what the killer used to subdue Rudy. The man was in good shape and could put up a fight." He motioned to Hardy who produced an evidence bag and sealed the four inch long bottle inside.

The county troops arrived. The assistant ME looked at the scene a moment, then told them to cut down Rudy. They put him on the floor on his back and the ME knelt in front of him. After a quick examination he looked at Chief Sanderson.

"Preliminary for the cause of death could be strangulation or those nails in his heart depending which one did it. I'll call that later."

Forensics took over. They bewailed the dozens of footprints in the chalky substance on the floor. They booted everyone out of the death room and went to work.

Downstairs, Hardy watched one of the forensic guys go through the stolen pickup truck.

"Oh yeah," the county man said holding up a medium sized plastic Pepsi cup. "We'll get DNA and maybe some prints off this." He bagged it and went on searching.

Chief Sanderson called from the front door. "That's a stolen one, all right. Sheriff said it was reported taken from a shopping center parking lot two days ago."

Hardy talked to the clues man. "Can you vacuum the floor in front of the driver's seat? We're looking for a certain brand of cat litter."

"You guys are weird," the forensic man said. "Yeah, I'll vacuum up everything there right down to the last dust mote."

Hardy went inside and talked to one of the carpenters.

"How many nail guns you have on this job?" he asked.

The carpenter shrugged. "Depends on what stage the construction is in. This late in the job, maybe three or four."

"Can you find them all and bring them to one spot? We need to take a look at them."

"The killer actually drove sixteens into the boss's heart?"

"He did. Several times. Where are those guns?"

Five minutes later the carpenter laid out three of the power nail guns.

"All I could find. Should be one more. Sometimes Rudy keeps one in his truck."

"Will any of these fire those big sixteen penny box nails?"

"No. That's the one missing."

Hardy told the Chief who grunted. "We'll check his pickup if we ever find it. If the killer had that Chevy pickup for two days, there must be some good stuff in it. He can't be perfect all the time."

Hardy told the Chief about the Pepsi cup.

"Yeah, maybe, and maybe it belonged to the owner so we get his DNA. We'll see."

Hardy went back to the Chevy pickup in the parking area. The forensics man was grinning.

"Find something?" Hardy asked.

The forensic man laughed. "Oh, yeah. He is getting sloppy. Know how when you cough you bring something up and spit it out? Well, somebody did that in this pickup within a day or two. Whoever did it tried to clean it up, but did a bad job. I got plenty for a DNA. If it matches the Pepsi spit we might be getting somewhere."

"Anything else? Fibers, hair, blood?"

"Not that I could find. No prints, for damn sure. I'll keep looking."

Hardy told Sanderson who nodded. "Good, maybe we're getting somewhere. They found Rudy's pickup. I have one of the forensic guys waiting at that Ford of yours. Rudy's rig is parked at the Taco Grande on Main. You can't miss it."

Ten minutes later, Hardy and Jose from the forensics team parked next to the beat up pickup.

Al Turley grinned. "Yep, found her. Not too tough.
I haven't touched her yet."

Jose went to work in the meticulous manner that
forensics men did. First he checked it visually, went
over some construction items in the body and then went
back to the cab.

"We figure the killer drove it back here from the kill
site, so he wasn't in it more than ten minutes," Hardy
told Jose who nodded.

"What are you looking for?" Hardy asked.

"Fibers, maybe some strands of hair. We have a
DNA but another one would help. No litter or trash,
Rudy kept a clean cab."

Hardy's cell chimed. "Yeah?"

"Hardy, get back up here to Fir Avenue. All five of
the workers came to the job this morning. We need to
interview them. None of them is running, which
doesn't help us much. Another forensic man is driving
down there. Tell the guy on the pickup."

For the next two hours, Hardy questioned the
workers at the house. One was a Mexican with a green
card. Two were locals Hardy had seen around town. All
told about the same story. They knew of no one who
had a grudge against Rudy. Certainly no one who might
want to kill him. He paid his bills, he was fair with the
workers, and he turned out good houses. The interviews
were a total waste of time but had to be done. The
Chief talked to the other two workers and learned
nothing.

Chief Sanderson rubbed his forehead and scowled
at Hardy. "Does this killing tie in with the other two?

Do we have any common denominator? Anything at all? I sure don't see one."

Hardy leaned against the Chief's sedan. "Chief, we have three different types of victims. Maybe he is doing this on purpose to throw us off and not establish any common ground."

"Maybe. But why? These aren't murder to gain anything. No big robbery or schemes involved. Just three ordinary people who get murdered,"

Sergeant Phillips, the sheriff's man in charge of the forensics squad, motioned to the Chief.

"We better get down to Rudy's pickup. Jose says he's found something that could be important."

19

JOSE GREETED the three men who bailed out of the Chief's cruiser.

"Might be something and then again..."

"So what is it?" Chief Sanderson asked.

"I didn't notice it at first," Jose said pointing to the plastic evidence bag in his hand. The keys were still in the ignition. You know how you hold a key when putting it in the slot. I used tape and got a good print that looks like a thumb. It is over other edges of prints but it should be readable."

"Thought we decided he must have worn gloves," Hardy said.

"He probably did. I figure he drove back here, parked, turned off the engine, and from habit pulled out the keys. Most drives do that automatically. Then he looked at his hands. He didn't want to walk the street wearing the plastic gloves so he pulled them off and put them in his pocket. Then he saw the keys and put the ignition key back in the slot. If it happened that way, we should have a good thumb print on the killer."

The sheriff's sergeant in charge of the group waved at Jose.

"So don't sit around here. Take a car and get back to the lab and see if you can find a match."

"If this guy is a first timer, he probably will not have been printed," Chief Sanderson said. "But it's a good piece of evidence we can use downstream when we find a suspect."

"One more thing," Jose said. "Lots of chalk dust on the floor mat. Can't say who put it there. Could have been Rudy over the last week or so."

Chief Sanderson agreed. "Right, it's too thin. A lawyer would get it pitched out of court. Now if we find that same dust on the shies of a suspect, then it could come into play."

"Right. I'm gone to the lab," Jose said.

They were half way back to the death house when Sanderson's cell rang.

"Yeah, so?"

"Chief, it's Joanie. Just got a call from a woman who runs Mary Jane's Fine Dresses on Pacific. She says she had a strange customer this morning and wants to talk to you about it. It might be a lead to the Charlotte killing. A man in his forties ordered a white dress, almost a match for the one they found Charlotte in."

"Sounds interesting. Call her back and tell her that Officer Jones will be there within ten minutes."

Nine minutes later, Hardy Jones went into the best woman's wear store in town and was met by the owner, Mrs. Beluka.

"Officer Jones?"

"Yes, ma'am. You had a weird customer?"

"I did. We don't get many men buyers. This one

was a little strange. About forty or so, not well dressed. Needs a haircut and a bath. He said his niece was graduating from something and he wanted to get her a nice dress and shoes, the whole thing. He looked at what we have in stock for a girl her size, about five feet one inches. He didn't like any of my dresses."

"Was ne nervous, uncomfortable?"

"No, not any more than most men who come in."

"So he didn't seem suspicious?"

"Not at first but ten he looked through a catalog I have and picked out a dress that is a match for the one that poor girl was dressed in. That really got me to thinking. Then he said he wanted under things and shoes. I made out an order and took a deposit. He said he didn't want to give me his name. He wanted to be sure this was a secret until he gave her the presents. I told him I'd call Portland and have the dress here by tomorrow noon."

"We should meet this gentleman," Jones said. "He could be a copycat, or maybe the same man who killed Charlotte. You said he'd be back here tomorrow at noon?"

"That's right. The dress will come out here tomorrow morning on a special delivery."

"Mrs. Baluga, we appreciate this. We'll be here to welcome him. You're sure you don't know who he is?"

"Never seen him before."

"Did you see what he was driving?"

"Never thought to check. Sorry."

"That's all right. We'll be here in the morning."

Back at the headquarters, Hardy wrote out a complete report on the talk with Mrs. Baluga and the meeting set for noon the next day. He gave it to Chief Sanderson who read it quickly.

"Interesting. We grab him, question him, and if it seems reasonable we get a search warrant for his vehicle and apartment."

The Chief frowned. "You still owe me a report on Rudy's hanging. Sooner the better."

"Yes, sir."

Hardy did a report on his lap top, printed it out, and put in on the Chief's desk. Rudy's murder troubled him. Who would want to kill a nice guy like Rudy? The rest of the day he would be talking to friends and business people Rudy worked with. He would be surprised if he turned up any kind of leads. Rudy's death seemed like a black hole in space. It just gobbled up all of the good theories and clues. Maybe the print off the ignition key would provide some leads. He hoped.

Work had stopped on the Fir Avenue death hose Rudy was building. Hardy stopped by to see if anyone there knew any of the subcontractors Rudy used. He found Wes Hightower there closing up doors and making the place as burglar proof as he could.

"Talked to Rudy's wife. I've been Rudy's foreman on the job. She told me to close down the job until things got sorted out. She cried when we talked. She said give her a while to take care of things."

He had some books Rudy kept on the job that listed several subs. Hardy took down their names and phone numbers.

"Lots of things could get stolen here," Hardy said. "Might be a good idea to hire one of your workers here to be a night guard. Ten o'clock to daylight. Can't hurt. Rudy's wife will approve I'm sure." He paused. "You think of anything else that could point to the killer? Furious supplier? Distraught husband. Little green men? Anything"

Hightower shook his head. "Not a glimmer of an idea. I've been trying."

Hardy made a call from his patrol car and headed for Glen Electric, one of the subs. He was almost to the address when his cell chimed. He pulled to the curb and answered it. "Yes, Jose. Any news?" The call came from the county forensic office.

"Indeed my boy, indeed. Got a good print. Checked the state, federal the FBI. Not a hint of a match. At least we have one print we can hold and hope to match to a suspect."

"Yeah, right. Tough luck. I was hoping."

"Happens. Oh, I was so pumped up about the print I forgot to tell you I found some strange hairs from the stolen pickup. I've been working on them and best I can come up with is that they are cat hairs. Short cat hairs about an inch and a half long."

"Short hair domestic," Hardy said. "It's a general category of cats without any pedigree."

"Yeah what the book says. I called the guy who had his pickup stolen. He doesn't have a cat. So maybe we can assume our killer owns a cat?"

"Good guess. Another maybe for my list of clues. Thanks. Any more news?"

"Not that we've got to. Still a few things to check out from the house and the two pickups."

They signed off, Hardy started his rig, and angled for the electric contractor.

The boss at Glen Electric was out on a job. It was a three person operation. Two partners and an office girl.

Marilyn was in her thirties, married to one of the partners and blonde.

"Sorry Pete is out right now. He handled the work on Rudy's new house. What a shame. Who would want to kill Rudy Gomez?"

"Any problems between him and your company?" Hardy asked.

"No, no. Not a chance. He was one of the best guys we've ever worked with. Knew what he wanted, did the job quickly, and paid his bill on time. We liked Rudy. Just a damn shame he's gone."

They talked for a few minutes more and Hardy checked Glen Electric off his list.

He looked at the next name on his pad, Town and Country Plumbing. He'd used them twice to clean out some sink problems. A small alarm sounded on his watch. He looked at the dial. It was almost four thirty. The day had whizzed past on him. He just had time to make it to the Little League practice. No way could he be late after missing the last game.

20

THE NEXT MORNING Hardy showed up at the dress shop twenty minutes to twelve wearing slacks and a sport shirt. They didn't want to scare this man off, but they needed a close up look at him. Mrs. Beluka said bad news, the dress from Portland was back ordered. She had a phone call this morning and would have it within two days.

"So we'll play it by ear and see how he reacts. Try to get a phone number so you can call him when it comes in."

"I should be able to do that. I expect that he'll come early."

The tiny bell on the door tinkled and Hardy moved behind a tall rack of dresses. A woman came in the door and Mrs. Beluka waited on her, made the sale, and the woman left.

It was five minutes after twelve and Hardy was worried. Bob Young was two doors down in uniform and the Chief sat in his cruiser across the street. Had they spooked this guy already?

Just then the door chimed again and a man came in. Hardy took refuge behind the dress rack and studied the man. He was in his forties, poorly dressed, needed a shave, and his hair was on the wild side. He approached the counter.

"Hello, did the dress come in?"

"I'm sorry, it didn't. I had a phone call from Portland this morning. They promised me it would be here in two days. Will that be all right?"

The man scowled. "You said today. Damn. That won't allow me much travel time. Got to go to Seattle. Hell okay. It better come."

"I can call you as soon as it gets here. Could I have a phone number to reach you?"

"What? Phone number? Yeah, guess that would be a good idea"

Mrs. Beluka wrote down the number he gave.

"Oh, about the shoes and under things. I won't be needing those. Just the dress."

"I'm sure it will be here. I'll call the minute it comes in."

He frowned, nodded, and walked out the door.

Hardy spoke into his cell phone as soon as the door closed. "Stand down. He's okay in here. We have a telephone number."

The Chief's voice came back. "Right, and I also have his vehicle year and make and his plate. Joanie is checking right now with DMV to get his last known."

Hardy tanked the store owner and hurried outside. Bob Long met him and they went across the street to the Chief's unmarked cruiser. The top cop was not smiling.

Hardy told them about the man not wanting the

shoes and under garments. "Wonder what that means?" Hardy asked.

"Maybe he bought them somewhere else," Long said.

"So we get his name and last known address, we don't have enough for a search warrant," the Chie said. "He got in his rig, that Volkswagen van down there, other side of the street. The green one. Long, you get in our car and tail him. We're putting him on a twenty four hour watch starting now. Hardy, you go home and get some sleep. You relieve Young at midnight. Let's hope we can get something, anything incriminating about him so we can get a warrant."

The Chief's phone buzzed.

"Joanie? I'll put you on the speaker."

"Chief. Got that info you wanted. His name is Amos Urick. He's forty two, one speeding ticket, one DUI that he beat. It was a prescription medication. He lives at 139 Third Avenue. That's a four unit apartment. He drives a nineteen ninety four Volkswagen van."

"Damn, I was hoping for an FBI most wanted. Okay check that name for prints or DNA in all of the print banks we can use. Do it now."

"Right, Chief. I'm on it."

"He's getting in the van, Long. You better shag ass out of here. Don't lose him."

LATER THAT AFTERNOON, Ed Rathwood felt strange, antsy, and irritable. He left his office and went out the back door to the alley where he parked his Jeep that looked like a holdover from World War II. No top, windshield slanted out, nothing in back. It was his tearing around back roads and sometimes off road wheels.

Not much off road chance in the county unless you knew some farmer up in the foot hills. At least there were quite a few gravel roads left. He loved driving on gravel. Sliding around the corers, spitting out rocks as he gunned it. Maybe he should have been a race car driver.

Ahead in the road he saw a crested quail ushering her hatch of five or six little chicks across the road. Ed grinned, gunned the Jeep, and hit the screeching quail and her flock head on.

He bellowed out a raucous "Oh yeah," and looked behind where he saw feathers falling to the ground and the small bodies littering the road. Ed laughed.

"Damn little birds you should be more careful," he shouted into the deserted country. He felt better. Hell, he could do anything he wanted to do. He didn't worry about it. Take old Rudy. He was surprised when he knew he was going to die. Tough luck. It's just what I'm doing tonight.

For years he realized that his conscience never bothered him. It took him a long time to understand that he had no conscience. He could do anything he wanted to, as long as he wasn't caught. That was the key. Be pleasant with people, act nice in public, run his business to make a profit, and establish himself as a pillar of the community. Yeah, and then he could get away with murder.

So far three down and out. The cops were going crazy thinking they might have three different killers. He laughed out loud. He loved to confuse and baffle the cops. Most fun than he had had in years.

Next who was next? He hadn't decided.

In the road ahead he spotted a milk cow that must have broken through the flimsy fence along the road. She was too big to take on head first. Maybe a side swipe would put her down and hurting.

Just before he made his move, a boy on a bicycle came over a small rise and chased the cow off the road. He waved at the boy as he drove past. Probably just as well. That big an animal could have put a lot of dents in the old Jeep and might have snapped an axle.

He was deep in the foothills west of town now, with few people and fewer buildings. Ahead he spotted an old barn. One side sagged inward. He slowed then stopped. He parked the Jeep just off the gravel and walked twenty yards to the barn. Mostly fallen in. One side held a wide door and inside he found more than a dozen stacked bales of hay. Keep them out of the coming rains. It always rained in Oregon. He took out his pocket lighter and flicked it on and off.

Ed grinned and his eyes went a little wild as he bunched loose hay against the bales. He added some boards to the stack, lit the bottom of the lose hay, and stepped back.

The dry straw caught fire and the flames spread quickly. They crawled across the floor in more lose hay, then ignited the bales and sent smoke to the top of the old barn.

Ed figured it was time to go, slipped out the door, and closed it. No smoke had made it out of the barn by tie time Ed started the Jeep, turned it around, and headed back toward town. He stopped about a mile away. Smoke gushed from the barn and lifted straight up in the windless sky. Soon he could see flames jetting through the roof.

Ed chuckled as he drove back to town. He met no other cars on the gravel road until he was five miles away from the fire. He laughed. Yes, what a great drive. He felt better. More stable and more relaxed. He was ready for the other part of his life. As he remembered there was a meeting tonight of the barbershop committee. He couldn't miss that.

Maybe something terrible would happen. Ed snorted he could only hope.

Next? Who would be next? He had a short list of three more names. One of them had to be the best suited for the next little project. But which one? He would have to decide soon. His plan was for six bodies in six weeks. So far he was pretty well on schedule.

As he drove, he wondered if his mother had figured it out yet? She had enough clues. She knew him well enough. Knew him? Hell, she had trained, tutored, and directed him for years. Several times she had urged and directed him to do certain things that she was afraid to do herself. He had never been caught for any of them. Maybe he should just ask her if she knew who had killed the three people in town. He shook his head. No, too direct, to blatant. He'd have to be subtle. He looked at his watch. What time was that barbershop committee meeting called for?

21

KING BRODERSON CALLED the Forest Glen Barbershop Ballad Contest Committee to order at eight that evening in the library meeting room.

"First order of business is to find a replacement for Rudy. We're all saddened by his death but we have to move on. Any volunteers?"

Ed spoke up. "I can follow through on that. I think Rudy had already ordered the chairs. I'll double check and organize a crew to set them up in the gym."

"Good. We thank you, Ed. Now Grace, how are the entries coming along?"

Grace Douglas smiled. "Better than last year at this time. I checked just before I came over here and we have twenty four solid entries who have paid the entry fee. That almost guarantees that they will show up for the contest."

"Good news, Grace. We going to need any additional judges?" King looked around. Nobody spoke up.

Clarence Rider stood. He was head of the music

department at Forest Glen University in town and always contacted the judges.

"I've put in a new system this year for judging. I don't have all of the details worked out yet, but we actually will use fewer judges and more head to head competition. I think it will be exciting. So, I'm sure we can handle up to about forty entries with the judging system we have."

"Good news, Clarence. Now for the most important aspect. The money. Jake Vining is our man with the check book. How are we doing, Jake?"

"We do have a problem, King. Or rather, I guess that I have a problem. I checked my balance sheets three times, had my best bookkeeper go over them and I still can't explain it. The problem is the books show that we're $300 short on our deposits. I can't explain it. One deposit of $300 simply didn't clear the bank."

King frowned. "Not good news, Jake. Any idea what happened?"

"One deposit might have been lost in the trash somewhere. I might have dropped it on the way to the bank. I just don't know."

"Three hundred isn't going to shoot us down, Jake. You keep looking." King shrugged. "Hell it could happen to any of us. One time I misplaced a fifteen hundred deposit. We found it a month later where it had been put in an accounts paid file folder."

"Jake, don't worry about the loss," Ed said. "I'll bring you a check to cover it."

There was a round of applause.

"Good of you, Ed, but I still want to find it. When I do, I'll pay you back."

"Hey, don't worry about it," Ed said.

The rest of the meeting went smoothly and King adjourned it about twenty minutes later. All was ready for the contest now just four weeks off.

On the way to his car, Ed caught up with Dr. Mildred Warnick.

"Hey, Doc. You didn't say a word tonight."

"Nothing to bring up. How is that leg doing? You didn't come in for a bandage change."

"Leg hurts some, but I guess I deserve it for being so sloppy. You want to change the dressing tonight? We could do it at your place."

Mildred smiled in the faint light. "Yes, let's do that. Follow me home and park out front."

Ten minutes later in her apartment, Dr. Warnick motioned for him to drop his pants.

"Just my pants? I could take down my briefs too."

"Hey, let me do my job here. We'll see about the briefs later." She had him sit on a kitchen chair, took off the bandage, and checked the wound critically.

"All right. Starting to heal. You were lucky, you know that. That bullet missed an artery by about half an inch. If it had torn that one open, you would have bled out on my front porch and been dead meat."

"Always have been lucky," Ed said.

She put some ointment on the wound then bandaged it again. When she finished she put away her black bag and nodded.

"Now, patient, if you will pull up your pants so you can walk we'll go into the bedroom and I'll check out your briefs. There seems to be a rather large bulge there that needs to be examined." A short time later in the bedroom they examined each other. Ed never did get home that night.

22

THE PREVIOUS AFTERNOON and evening Officer Bob Young followed the suspect in his VW bus. He had stopped by at the bowling alley and rolled three games. He wasn't good Young decided as he watched four lanes down the way.

Amos Urick wasn't happy with his bowling. He quit the third game half way through and turned in his shoes.

Outside he sat in his VW for two or three minutes before he drove away. He went back to the address they had for him, parked, and went inside. It was the last Officer Young saw of Urick that night, He tuned the stake out over to Hardy at midnight.

Hardy had come prepared with two sandwiches, a thermos of coffee and four donuts,

It was a long night. He turned on the radio to a classical music station and waited with Vivaldi, Brahms, and Van Cliburn. Nobody left the front door of the four apartment building. He didn't know if there was a back entrance. The VW bus didn't move.

At daylight, Hardy got out of the patrol car and walked around the VW bus. He looked in the passenger side window and yelped out loud. On the passenger's side seat he saw laid out a white bra and white panties and a pair of gold colored flat shoes.

Hardy didn't hesitate he dialed the Chief's home phone. The top cop came on sounding grumpy.

"Yeah, so who is it?"

"Hardy, Chief. You won't believe what I just saw." He told Sanderson about the clothes on the front seat. "This with the white dress order, is it enough for a search warrant?"

"Could come close. Depends on which judge we talk to. You hang there until eight and I'll have a relief for you. Meantime I'm calling the DA in Hillsboro and see what he thinks. He might go along. He wants this guy as bad as we do. Hang tough. If Urick moves you stay with him and let us know where you are. Out."

Hardy went back to his private car and got in. No sense spooking Urick now. He watched the four unit apartment house. No way to tell which one Urick was in.

It was another long wait until eight when Al Turley showed up in an unmarked car. He parked behind Hardy. They talked for a minute and Hardy updated him on the clothes in the bus.

"Could be a copycat," Turley said.

"I hope not," Hardy said. "I'm heading back to the station. The chief talked to the DA. Don't know what is happening. My guess is we'll get a warrant for his apartment and his bus. See you later."

Hardy waited at the police station and about nine o'clock the Chief came in.

"Good, you're still here. Take a drive to Hillsboro to that address, it's where Judge Vanderpelt lives. He's got a search warrant waiting for you. I got it to cover anything relate to the three murders including clothes."

"Great news, Chief. I'm on my way.

AN HOUR later he Chief and three officers parked in front of the Urick apartment. Urick answered the door of the lower right apartment.

Surprise flooded his face. "Hey, three cops. What is this all about?"

"Are you Amos Urick?"

"Yes."

"We have a warrant to search your van and your apartment. Please step outside, now."

"What is this about?"

"Just step outside and don't interfere," Chief Sanderson said.

Hardy took the VW bus to search. It wasn't locked. He checked the girl's clothing. It was all new with sales slips in bags in the back of the bus. He found nothing that would tie Urick to any of the killings. A lot of fast food wrappers, a library book that was overdue, thee ticket stubs to movies, and a check stub showing that he had worked for three days on a construction job.

Hardy checked for any sign of concealed panels but found nothing. He looked in the engine compartment and underneath. Nothing. He went inside the apartment.

The Chief and Officer Doug Olson had finished their search job. The Chief shrugged.

"Not a damn thing that shouldn't be here. Nothing

to tie him to any of the killings. No wall full of mementoes from the killings. No tacked up newspaper clippings. He looks clean."

Outside a woman drove up, parked, and hurried up to the apartment. Officer Olson stopped her at the front door.

"What is going on here?" she asked. She was a large woman with a big voice and about forty.

"We have a legal search warrant to look over this apartment and Mr. Urick's van."

"For goodness sakes. Amos is harmless. Just a little lazy. Why would you search his place?"

The Chief came out, told the woman about the girl's under things and shoes and about the dress.

The woman smiled. "Really? Good for him. He said he was going to have a surprise for Janet. It's her sixteenth birthday and we plan a surprise outing and dinner for her. I'm pleased he's going to the effort to get the things."

"We found nothing incriminating," the Chief said. "Sorry we bothered you. You're free to go in the apartment now."

The Chief waved and the officers hurried back to the Chief's cruiser.

"So much for what looked like a good suspect," the Chief said. "Now what the hell else do we have to work on?"

Back at the station, Hardy went over the board again, checking each clue on each of the three cases. He came up with only a few common clues, and they were pretty general. What they needed was a breakthrough. An eye witness to one of the killings would be ideal.

A woman came into the station a half hour later and Joanie called Hardy.

"There's a Miss Shannon McGuire here to see you. She with the Times-News. Wants an interview on the three killings."

Hardy had a notion to say he was too busy, but then he thought a good story in the local weekly paper might jog somebody's memory. He told Joanie to send her in.

He met her in the hall and they went into interview room number one. He didn't want her looking at the tack board with all of their clues and information on it.

They traded names, she gave him a card with her phone number on it, and he gave her one of his cards.

She was in her twenties, short dark hair, a pretty face with big brown eyes, and a slender body. She had a sly smile and he liked her at once.

"Now, Miss McGuire what can I do for you?"

"Tell me that you have a hot suspect and will solve the three murders this week."

Hardy laughed. "Yes, that would be a good news story. Probably make the front page. Afraid I can't do that."

"Tell me what you can about your investigation. We know a lot about the victims, but almost nothing about any clues or leads that you might have."

Hardy clicked open and closed his ball point pen.

"Yes, we have some leads, not many, but a few. I can tell you we are almost certain that the killer is a man. We don't know if he's local or from out of town, or just passing through on a murderous rampage."

"May I quote you on that, Officer Jones?"

"You may if you'll call me Hardy."

"I will. I'm Shannon."

"I can say that we believe there is one man who has struck three times. We don't know why he picked these particular victims. We can't establish any kind of a pattern that would help us. I can say that I believe the killer is intelligent, crafty, and seems to know a lot about Forest Glen. I'm not a psychiatrist but it does look like this killer could be a psychopath."

Shannon looked up from a lap top on which she had been taking notes. "If I remember right, a psychopath is a person who has absolutely no conscience and does exactly what he wants to do no matter who it hurts. He simply doesn't care about anyone or anything but his own emotions and desires."

"That's about it. Which makes him that much harder to catch since we have no pattern and no idea of his projected behavior or activities."

"Do you think there is any connection between Willy's death and the murder of Charlotte Alberts?"

"The only thing in common between them is that they were both students at Forest Glen High. We don't think there is any other common element."

"What about Rudy Gomez?"

"Around here all we can say is who would want to kill a nice guy like Rudy? We are absolutely at a loss."

"Has the forensics lab men from the sheriff's department been of any help on the cases?"

"Yes, they have. They always can find more than we who are not trained in that field. But so far we have nothing that would make a case against any killer."

She typed in some more notes on her lap top then looked up.

"One last question. Do you think the killer will

strike again and murder someone else here in Forest Glen?"

"I can't answer that, Shannon. Only the killer knows what he's going to do. And he hasn't told me any of his plans."

"What a good answer. That takes care of all my questions. May I call you from time to time about any news on the cases?"

"Certainly, Shannon McGuire. Anytime at all."

23

THAT SAME AFTERNOON Ed's leg hurt so much that he wanted to scream. He took three Tylenol, but they didn't touch the pain. He called Dr. Warnick and got through to her between patients.

"Leg hurts like it's still on fire, Doc. Can you get me some pain pills?"

She suggested Tylenol but he said they hadn't helped.

"It's four thirty," she said. "You be here at five and we can talk and I'll give you some of my private stock of knock out pain pills."

"I'll be there, If I can stand it another half hour."

All the patients had been treated and the office nurse had just left when Ed walked into Dr. Warnick's office. She heard the door and came out.

"So the pain finally came," she said. "Pain has a strange way of acting sometimes. Come on back to my office and we'll get you doped up good."

"Thanks, I appreciate this."

In her office he swallowed two potent pain pills and

she told him to sit down so she could see if they would give him any adverse reaction.

"Sometimes they can make a person faint."

He sat down and she looked at him with a strange smile.

"I think I know something nobody else in town knows. It's about your gunshot. I didn't hear about anyone else around here being shot. I called the police and asked them if they had any reports of gunshot wounds during the past week."

"Hey, what is this, the third degree? I think it's time I get out of here."

"No, not yet. There's the gunshot and then your wanting that small bottle of chloroform to put your cat to sleep. Somehow things began coming together."

"I don't know what you're driving at. I told you it was an accident with one of my guns. I have a collection of over a hundred fire arms."

"Call it a woman's intuition. You got that gunshot wound the same night that Rudy Gomez died."

"So?"

"Interesting. You know I started my studies to be a psychiatrist. I know a lot about abnormal psychology."

"You saying I'm a nut case?"

"Not saying anything. Just wondering about some circumstances. Then I treated your mother yesterday. She's a big talker. Mostly she talked about you and how proud she is of you and how you've taken over the store and now building a new one."

"So, again?"

"Oh we talked about a lot of things. She said she worries about you. About how sometimes you seem unattached to your life outside the store. She said now and then it seems like your conscience isn't quite responding right to things."

"Sounds like two women gossiping," Ed said. "Got to get out of here and make one more check on those extra chairs for the Barbershop Ballad contest. About that my conscience is clear."

As they talked she had him pull down his pants so she could check his wound. She took off the old bandage and checked the gunshot then re-bandaged it. He stood and pulled up his pants and fastened them.

"Can I get out of here now?"

"Sure. Just tell me that you didn't have anything to do with Rudy's murder."

"That's such an insulting question that I won't even answer it. Not kind of you at all, Doc. I better leave before I have time to get mad at you."

"Yes, you're right. But you still didn't answer my question."

Ed glared at her threw two twenty dollar bills on the counter and slammed the outside door when he left.

Dr. Mildred Warnick let her frown grow. He hadn't answered her. He hadn't denied it. But then neither did he admit it. She put away her instruments and closed up the office. That was when she decided that she would never be alone again with Ed Rathwood no matter how good he was in bed.

WHEN THE TIMES-NEWS came out the next morning, Hardy saw with surprise his picture on the front page along with a long story about the three murders. For the first time the paper called them serial killings. Shannon had quoted him accurately and gave background on the three victims.

Chief Sanderson marched up to Hardy's desk and threw the newspaper down.

"Why didn't you clear this with me before you began shooting your mouth off to a reporter?"

Hardy stood. "Chief, never have had to check with you before when a reporter asked questions. You weren't here, or I would have had her talk to you."

The Chief slumped in the guest chair beside Hardy's desk. "Hell, maybe it won't matter. You didn't give up any of our meager clues. It could just smoke somebody out who knows something or saw something the nights off the killings."

"That's what I was hoping, Chief."

"We'll just have to wait and see. Oh, one thing more. The paper has put you in a spotlight about the case. Our killer might not like that. He might take a bead on your skull with a forty five automatic. I want you to be alert, to cover you tail at all times, and not give this bird a good shot at you unless he's using a thirty ought six with a ten power scope."

Hardy thought about that for a few seconds then shook his head. "Chief, I'm just small potatoes here. He won't give me a passing thought. Probably hard at work picking out his next victim right now."

"Yeah, so make certain it isn't you, Jones."

24

ED COULDN'T REMEMBER when he had been so angry. He was furious. He felt like burning down the whole town. He thought he had something special going with Doc Warnick. At least she was outstanding in bed. She must get lots of practice.

She accused him of killing Rudy. How? Okay, she had special knowledge that no one else did. She put chloroform and a bullet wound and the date together and made her conclusion.

No one else in town could do the same. He checked his watch. A little after five thirty. He had a date with a university professor, even though the academic didn't know it. The man's name was Dr. Clarence P. Rider. Head man in the music department at the university and head of the judges for the barbershop contest. He was a glorious overachiever. He had to pay. The man had a meeting with his various section heads tonight, but it wouldn't start until eight o'clock.

Ed had put in four days tracking the professor and recording his movements. He usually came home from his office at the university about three, took a nap, and had an early dinner. Most evenings he spent back at the university for meetings, some private tutoring, and other garbage.

Ed parked his new Lexus a half block from the professor's house and waited.

He couldn't put the idea that Doc Warnick had made such an accusation. He had been pondering just what to do since he left her office. The solution was so obvious he had a hard time accepting it.

Dr. Mildred Warnick would be the next person to be honored on his overachiever roster. It would have to be soon, before she got thinking about her clues too much, and went to the police. Not tonight. He needed some time to plan and prepare. He'd do it tomorrow night.

He knew her routine already. She had told him several times her best hours were from five to seven when the office was empty and she could review her patients for the day, do research, and just relax. Getting in would be easy.

He started the car and headed home. Tonight he would do his planning and getting reedy. A sudden grin broke out across his face. Yes, he knew how he would do it: appropriate, fitting. This one would really upset the local cops.

When he got home, he stopped in the living room. The local weekly newspaper lay on the coffee table. He glanced at it. He subscribed to it as a courtesy to a fellow local business man, the publisher. The headline stopped him:

Police Making Progress
On Serial Killings Here

He saw a picture of a cop with the story. He read the first paragraph.

"Police Officer Hardy Jones said that the department is making progress in tracking down the serial killer who has struck three times in the past month. Officer Jones said they know the killer is a man but they are not sure if he is local or someone just passing through."

Ed scowled. Who the hell was this cop and what did he really know? Ed made a mental bill board in his brain to keep tabs on this cop. He could prove to be too smart for his own good. But that would have to come later. He had two prospects now.

He spent the rest of the evening working out his plans for the good Dr. Warnick.

THE NEXT MORNING, King Broderson and Ed walked the construction site of the shopping center.

"Foundations are all in and cured," King said. "Got the slab poured yesterday. Look at that bitch. I never thought it was going to be this huge. Looks different on paper."

They went down two hundred feet and Ed had a chance to look over his new building site. They were still pouring the foundations.

"What in hell am I going to do with all of this space?" Ed asked as he stared at the outlines of his new store adjacent to King's new supermarket.

"No sweat little buddy. You'll fill it up in a week and ask if you can put in some warehouse space."

"Not a chance. But I do have to talk with Uriah and

start making some orders for delivery. They gave me a three month completion date."

"Don't believe them. They promised me two months but already they are baking off on that."

It was almost eleven o'clock before the two were finished. They both had talked to the foremen. King had to make a change in materials, since what he had wanted wasn't available.

A catering truck wheeled in and flipped up its side so it could serve food and drinks. Eleven was lunch time for the crew and the catering truck was swamped. Ed and King had cups of coffee and headed for their cars.

"I check in two or three times a week," King said. "Keeps them on their toes. You should come out and look around more often."

"Got to do that," Ed said. They waved and headed back to town in their own cars. On the quick drive, Ed refined his plans for Doc Warnick. This was Thursday, not her bridge night. She had told him about the bridge group they had and how they had been shut down from offering a "prize" for the winner. He had laughed for five minutes.

"Lucky you didn't get splattered all over the newspapers. The national TV news programs would have eaten it up."

"And I'd be though as a doctor here in town," he said. "We all appreciated how the police handled it."

He put that out of his mind and went over his plans again. Just after five at her office. He'd wait until he was sure that the last of her worker bees had left. Then he'd ring the bell and pound on the door until she came. He wouldn't let her see him though. She might be scared the way he yelled at her yesterday. Oh, yes, it would be a good kill. He would get a thrill, a surge of excitement watching her. He decided that he would let her stay conscious through the whole thing right up to the last minute. He wasn't sure how fast the drug would act, but he'd make sure to use enough. The more he thought of it, the better his mood became.

At the store, he called Uriah in and they began planning on what new lines they would order for the new store. Already Uriah had seen plans for the new layout and had sketched in various displays he thought would be appropriate.

"We don't want to look jammed full of goods like the discount furniture stores are," he said. "We need to maintain a dignity and class, but still offer a lot more lines and displays tan we do now."

They worked most of the afternoon, and then Ed realized that he had some tasks to take care of before his five o'clock date with Doc Warnick.

He hurried home and went to the work shack in the back part of the woods and opened the doors. Inside was the l986 Chevy sedan he had repainted a dull brown. It was the one he had used to pick up Willy a month ago. It now looked nothing like it had then. It would pass as just another junker. He'd use it to drive near her office and park it. He put a pair of riot cuffs in his backpack along with some sticky tape. Everything else he needed would be in Doc Warnick's office. He smiled. This one would serve two purposes. The most important one was silencing a voice that could betray him to the police.

At four thirty he drove out the gate at home in the old brown Chevy and down half a block from the doctor's office. He parked where he could see the office door. Promptly at five o'clock her nurse left. A short time later the office girl opened the outside door then talked for a moment to someone inside before she left.

Ed waited another five minutes. No one else left. He carried his backpack and walked casually toward the doctor's office. He wore a dark checkered blue shirt and jeans. Nobody would think him out of place.

Ed went up the sidewalk to the office front door, rang the bell, and then he pounded hard six times on the door. He waited. He heard movement inside and grinned. It wouldn't be long now.

25

HARDY TRIED NOT to think about it. He knew that the Chief had gone overboard. Why would the serial killer target him? It was ludicrous. Just because of that little story in the newspaper? Ridiculous. Now the Chief said he had to call in to Joanie every hour on the hour no matter what he was doing whenever he was away from the station.

He had written two tickets that morning for flagrant violations of the city speed laws. Now he was on a domestic dispute call. There was something that could be dangerous. Say the man is beating up on his wife. You try to restrain the man and the woman is all over you clawing and scratching and telling you to leave her man alone.

No such trouble on this call. The man had taken off before Hardy got there. He took a report from the woman, who said they were estranged, and the man had come back to get a TV set he said was his. He took it and left.

Hardy's watch chimed and he saw it was two

o'clock. He went back to his patrol car and used the radio to call Joanie.

"Joanie, this is 22 and I'm still here, hale and hearty, and no big bad guy has captured me."

"Good. Keep it that way. Oh, the Chief said you should start changing any routine things you do. If you have lunch at one café all the time, you should move around to a different one each day. Same thing about driving to work. Don't use the same route each day. Vary it by going out of your way."

"Joanie, why is the Chief so worried about this?"

"Next time in the station, I'll tell you. Stay well."

They signed off and Hardy went back to making a patrol of the south part of town where most of the low income houses were.

He finished his shift just before five and sat down in the chair next to Joanie's desk.

"So, the Chief?"

She answered a phone call then turned to him.

"It happened in Portland before the Chief came out here. He had a partner who got a lot of publicity in the Oregonian newspaper about a series of arrests he made in a huge car theft ring. They had been stealing high end luxury cars and shipping them all over the world. A fifty thousand dollar Lincoln here could be sold for a hundred grand in Japan or in the oil rich nations. He stopped it cold. He testified at the trial that put away six of the kingpins. The next day he was shot dead outside his house as he left for work. The killer was never found.

"That's why the Chief is worried. You are not to talk to any newspaper or TV reporter until this is all over."

"Wow. I never heard that story. At least now I know why he's so touchy about it."

"I had a call this morning from a TV reporter from Portland wanting to set up a video interview with you. I told them that you were not available. This woman reporter was unhappy."

"Thanks. I promise to be extra careful for the next week or so. Either we catch this guy or he leaves town. Right now I hope we catch him."

Hardy didn't tell his wife about the Chief's concern. She did ask about his sudden change in shift days and times. He worked fewer nights, and had different days off. He told her it was just a normal changing around of shifts.

After the talk with Joanie, he was more careful. On his way home he took a different route. He backed his car into the driveway for a quick getaway if needed. Now he made sure that the blinds were down in the house after dark. He told himself he was just taking practical precautions.

ED POUNDED on Doc Warnick's door again and this time he heard a faint voice.

"I'm closed. Who is it?"

"UPS, with a delivery you have to sign for," Ed said, changing his voice just enough to conceal his identity.

"Just a minute."

He heard locks being opened. Then the door was unlatched and moved an inch inside. Ed had taken a step back and now he surged forward, hitting the solid door with his shoulder, slamming it forward.

He saw Doc Warnick jump out of the way.

"You're not...." she began. Then she screamed. He grabbed her, pushed his hand over her mouth, and slammed her against the wall. Then he closed the outside door.

"Enough of the protest, Doc. You and me gonna have ourselves a good little talk." He kept his hand over her mouth and forced her to walk through the waiting area and back to the first examining room. It had most of what he needed. Ed kicked the door shut and dropped her into a chair. She screamed again. He slapped her hard with his open hand and her eyes went wide with surprise and pain. She stopped screaming.

"Why? What are you doing?"

"Self-preservation. Checkmating a possible danger to me. Prevention is the best defense."

"Oh, my God. Then I was right. You did kill Rudy Gomez. Oh, my God. I was only guessing. I didn't know for sure. I would not have gone to the police with what I knew."

"You should have told me that yesterday. Too fucking late now. What a shame. You are so good in bed. I should fuck you hard and fast right now, but I really don't have the time."

Dr. Mildred Warnick stared at him in shock and disbelief. She was suddenly so frightened that she shivered. Surely he couldn't mean what he had indicated. She had never been so terrified in her life. What could she do to talk him out of his plans? Strip for him? He'd like that. He always loved her breasts. A rage shook her. She sprang from the chair, grabbed a scalpel from the counter, and charged him.

He slapped her away and she crashed into the examination table. His fist pounded hard against her right wrist knocking the blade away. He put both hands around her throat and lifted her off the floor.

"I could just strangle you, but that would be no fun at all. Too common. We need something more sophisticated and classy. Which is why you're going to open up your drug locker for me. You do it right now." He let her down so she stood on the floor.

"No. It's a combination lock and I won't tell you what it is."

He grabbed the scalpel from the floor and held it in front of her right eye.

"Ever thought of being blind, Doc? One little stab and your eye won't ever see a thing again. You want that?"

"You wouldn't do that. Doesn't all the great times we had in bed mean anything to you?"

"Not a thing. A thrill for the moment. Now, nothing. Let's go to the locker."

He forced her out of the room and down to the end of the hall where he had seen her get drugs before. It was a two foot square box sitting on a table and bolted to the wall. He pushed her in front of it.

"Open it."

"No."

The small, sharp blade slashed out and sliced a four inch wound down her left arm.

She bellowed in pain and reached for a towel to stop the blood. He didn't let her get it.

"Open the box or I cut you again."

She looked at him with a new respect for his cruelty, his lack of compassion. Then she knew. He had no conscience, none at all. He was a psychopath and now on a killing rampage while acting like a pillar of the small town. Nothing would stop him. She closed her eyes, shook her head in sadness, then reached up and turned the dial on the drug cabinet lock. She finished and pulled the door open. Then she took a towel off the bench and wrapped it around her arm.

Ed stared at the drugs. Not a lot but he saw what he needed: ampoules of morphine, individual shots the doctor could administer the way Marine medics did in combat. He grabbed a handful and pushed them into his pocket.

When he turned around, Doc Warnick had taken off her blouse and bra. "How about one more fuck for old time's sake?" she asked. "You win both ways."

Ed watched her. Was she trying something? Was she plotting how to get away? He didn't see how. He pushed her down the hall to an exam room.

"On the exam table," he said a touch of passion showing in his voice. "Come on."

They went into exam room two without any blood on the floor.

"Get out of the rest of your clothes," he said.

Doc Warnick's mind was whirling. How could she hurt him? She remembered one of the doctors she worked with said every woman doctor should have an ice pick hidden in each exam room. Under the thin matt on the table would be a good place. For years she had hidden ice picks there. Was there one under this thin mattress? She always kept them on the side of the table nearest her.

"Hey, get those clothes off."

She slid out of the skirt she wore and shoes and then her panties.

"On the table, Doc, you know the routine."

When he saw her naked and sitting on the table, he turned around and pulled down his pants and boxer shorts.

As he did she searched for the ice pick. Glory! She found it, pulled it out, and lay down on her back on the table with her hands over her head. That way she could hide the ice pick.

Ed kicked off his pants and shorts and knelt on the table between her legs. As he did his hands were at the sides supporting himself, and she half way sat up and stabbed the ice pick at his genitals. The first stab went through his scrotum. He screeched in pain and swiped at her hand holding the six inches of sharp steel spike.

He missed and she stabbed twice more both times daggering through his erection and dumping him off the exam table. She sat up then wielding the ice pick like a saber.

Ed had hit the floor hard, but now sat up and screeched in pain. A moment later he surged upward, slapped the ice pick from her hand, and then his fist jolted into her jaw slamming her back hard on the table.

He hovered over her his face a mask of hatred. "You bitch, you fucking whore. I had almost relented to let you live but not now. Now you are going to die a thousand times. You'll beg me to put you out of your misery." He hung over her his face showing the pain in his genitals. It was a burning, stabbing pain that almost knocked him out. He held on and beat down the pain as far as he could.

He picked up a scalpel from a cabinet. "The Chinese have a name for it—'The Death of a Thousand Cuts.' No one cut will let you bleed enough to die. But even a hundred will bleed you out a little at a time.

Then, when you're so weak you can hardly breathe, I'll give you the final coup de grace."

He tied her hands with the plastic riot cuffs. She was still so stunned by the hit in the face that she could barely move.

The table had restraining straps. He fastened the one around her stomach and took up the little knife. Before he made any cuts he taped her mouth closed, then he slashed a four-inch slice down her right thigh. Blood flowed and dripped onto the white paper on the table. She tried to scream at the gush of pain but nothing left her throat. This was going to take some time he knew. But he had all night. He lifted the blade again and cut her other thigh.

26

THE NEXT MORNING Officer Bob Young had taken the call from a frantic nurse at Dr. Warnick's office at 7:45. Hardy and Chief Sanderson arrived at her office about ten minutes later.

Hardy took a quick look inside the examining room and hurried outside for some fresh air. He'd nearly lost his breakfast. Never in his life had he seen such a bloody scene. Dr. Warnick lay on her back on the exam table with slashes and stabs and cuts over so much of her body that blood covered her from neck to toes. There must have been more than fifty slashes and slices Hardy figured. So much rage and anger had come surging out from the killer.

Her face had been spared but it showed a mask of terror and pain. It was a slaughter. The Chief came out a few minutes later. He used his cell and notified the county sheriff's department about the homicide and requested their forensics team to come.

Almost an hour later the sheriff kicked the sidewalk. "She must have bled to death. So why the morphine?"

"Morphine?"

"Yeah. I didn't notice it at first. Young pointed them out. Ten ampoules of morphine had been stabbed into her chest. They are the kind the military medics use on the battlefield. One cuts down pain. Ten would kill almost anyone in a rush. Maybe she didn't die fast enough for the killer.'

Hardy got his stomach under control and went back into the death room. Blood everywhere, splattered on the walls, ceiling, and the floor as if the killer was spreading it around for effect.

He looked at her chest just above her mutilated breasts. The one shot morphine ampoules had been left untouched by the blood. The killer wanted to be sure police saw them. Hardy began taking notes. He should have his lap top to do this the way the reporter did.

After he put down a description of the room and the blood, position of the body and anything else he thought important, he stood in one place near the door and looked around the small room for any clues he might find. At first he saw nothing unusual. The normal medical supplies were there but scattered.

Why the Doc? Hardy thought. She was the second best medic in town. Two of the doctors were about ready to retire. Why Doc Warnick?

He checked the floor. In his rampage, maybe the killer had dropped something. A driver's license would be helpful. In the far corner almost hidden by a stack of tumbled white towels that must have fallen off a shelf, he saw what looked like the straps of a backpack. Might be something. He pointed it out to the Chief.

"He's getting sloppy. Yeah, has to be a backpack probably used that on each of his kills, but forgot it this time. This must have been an emotional binge for him to forget the pack"

"Forensics will have a field day with that, if it's his. How can we tell? It could be left by a patient, or maybe part of the Doc's gear."

"Don't think so. Whoever cleans up before they go home would have found it and put it in the lost and found box."

Outside they put yellow crime scene tape up around the entrance. So far they had talked to four people who tried to come to work. All were horrified. Young took their names and phone numbers after quick interviews. None of them had any idea who might have wanted to harm their doctor. The office was in a row of small businesses. All but two of them closed at five o'clock. Hardy called on the other two that stayed open until eight.

"Sorry, didn't see a thing unusual last night," the manager of an ice cream store across the street said. "What's going on over there?"

"You sure you didn't see anyone prowling around or knocking on the Doc's door? I know she stays late some nights."

"Like I said, didn't notice nothing out of the ordinary. Sometime the Doc stops by for a milkshake or a sundae. But not last night. What happened?"

"Somebody killed Doc Warnick."

"My God. Really? Who would want to hurt a nice lady like the Doc?"

"That's what we're trying to find out," Hardy said. He checked the other retail shop that sold cosmetics, but the woman owner told him the same thing. She hadn't seen anyone or any car that looked out of place.

Hardy told the Chief about his talk with the merchants.

"Figures. He could have come anytime posing as a patient. Or maybe after the help had left and she was there alone but before she went home. He must have known her habits."

"He always does."

The County Sheriff's forensics team arrived and went to work. The assistant Medical Examiner was busy and would get there as soon as he could. This time they brought a photographer who took pictures of the exam room from a dozen different angles and close ups on the body.

Before the photo man was done, Chief Sanderson took a call on his cell. It was Joanie from the station.

"He found what, Joanie?"

"He's a floor finisher at the house Rudy was building. They got the go ahead to complete it. He said he found a gouge in the hardwood floor in the entrance area. He cleaned the spot and says there's the end of a bullet sticking out of the wood. He says he is a shooter and knows what a lead slug looks like. He wonders if it's important."

Chief Sanderson nodded. "Could be. I'll send one of the forensic men over there. Thanks."

Ten minutes later Hardy pulled his cruiser to a stop in front of Rudy Gomez's last house. The Chief had made him chauffeur for the forensic man.

Jose met them at the front door.

"Glad you got here. Hope it helps. I know Rudy had a gun he carried most of the time, a little .22 automatic. This slug looks like a .22."

He opened the door and showed them the spot.

The forensic man grinned. "Sure as hell it is. I've got to dig it out. Will that matter?"

"Hell, no. Not if it will help nail the bastard killer. I can put in a new board."

Jose brought a half inch wide wood chisel and a small hammer and cut a square around the slug. Then he drove the chisel under the side and popped out the two inch square of flooring that held the slug.

"Perfect," the forensic man said. "Thanks. We'll take this back and test it for lines and grooves. Make a record. If a .22 caliber pistol shows up, we could have a match."

Back at the doctor's office, the ME had come and said he could give no preliminary cause of death.

"Could have been she bled out. Or it could have been the damn morphine. I'll be able to tell in the lab."

The forensic men had taken over but admitted they had little to go on. The Chief pointed to the corner where the white towels lay that were mostly covered with blood. They dug into the pile and found the backpack.

"Well now," the team lead said. "Do we know if it's his?"

"Not a clue," the Chief said.

They took it out to the sidewalk and looked inside.

"Well, now," the forensic guy said. "Sticky tape, pliers, three of those ampoules of morphine, a black baseball cap, and a small bottle labeled as chordophone. Bet we can get some good prints off that little bottle."

Hardy told the Chief about the .22 slug they dug out. "Jose said that Rudy usually carried a small .22 automatic with him. Chances are he tried to shoot the killer. Hope he hit him."

"Check with the other doctors in town and with the hospital in Hillsboro for any gunshot wound patients. Phone should work."

Hardy took off for the police station and the Chief told Bob Young he was back on call and patrol. Nothing more they could do at the kill site.

Hardy made his calls to the local doctors. He knew most of them and their staffs. None of them had had any gunshot patients in the last three weeks. He called the Sheriff's Office in Hillsboro. Yes, they had a gunshot patient reported by a local doctor. The victim was a visitor from Arizona showing off how fast he could draw and shoot. He outdid himself on one shot and it dug a groove down his right leg. He was shooting a .38 with a four inch barrel. It was two weeks ago and the man had left for Arizona a week later.

Hardy wrote a report. Later he would put in on his computer, print it out, put a copy on the Chief's desk, and put one up on the clues board. He also would work up a spot on the board for Dr. Mildred Warnick.

He thought about the four killings. Still no common denominator. Nothing to tie down the killer. Still it had to be the same man. That thirtyish man the witness had seen pick up Willy.

His phone chattered at him.

"Hardy, Joanie. Been a three-car crash right in the middle of town at Pacific and Main. Better get over there and see what you can do."

The intersection was blocked. Hardy found two volunteers to direct traffic a block away around the mess. Then he called two tow trucks and made sure all the drivers got names and addresses from the other ones. The youngest of the lot was a bit unsteady on his feet. Hardy gave him two field sobriety tests and made him walk the white line. He flunked them all. Hardy hand cuffed him and put him in the back of the patrol car. He'd get a breath test at the station, but Hardy knew he was far too drunk to be driving.

By the time he got back to the station and booked the drunk driver, it was nearly noon. Joanie called him.

"Man on line two wants to talk to a real policeman," she said. "You're elected."

"Yes, sir. This is Officer Hardy Jones. How can I help you?"

"You a real cop?"

"As real as they get off TV," Hardy said.

"Good, I need to talk to you. Can you come see me? I live upstairs in a store across from Doc Warnick's office. I heard about her. Dammed shame. But I might be able to help. I spend a lot of time looking out my window from my wheel chair. Yesterday just after five o'clock I saw a man go up to Doc Warnick's office door and pound on it hard, twice. That's when I took out my seven by fifty binoculars and zeroed in on him. He wore a black backpack which I thought strange. After he knocked he turned and pressed against the wall. That's when I saw his face. I'm almost certain that I know who the guy is."

27

HARDY CALLED the Chief and caught him just before he arrived home. He told him about the call from the window watcher.

"You know his name and address," the Chief said excitement creeping into his voice.

"Right, he's Ben Bascomb, and he lives over the ice cream store. He's the owner's father and they both live upstairs."

"Good, see you there in about ten minutes. Wait for me outside."

Hardy parked near the Glen Ice Cream Parlor and it was only two minutes before the Chief pulled up. They talked a minute then went inside the store that was still open.

"Gentlemen, what's your choice today," the owner asked.

"We had a call from your father. Mr. Bascomb said he saw something yesterday that might be important to the Doctor Warnick murder."

"Don't say. He's either watching out the window or

glued to his TV set. He's in a wheelchair you know. Be glad to take you upstairs. Let me lock the front door."

They went up a flight of stairs that led from the store room to the second floor. There were four rooms with only one facing the street.

They went into the front room and a man in a wheelchair looked up.

"Well officers, I'm Ben. Saw you drive up. You sure make good time. Not more than fifteen minutes ago I talked to the man at the station."

"That was me, Mr. Bascomb. Would you tell Chief Sanderson what you told me?"

Ben did with every detail the same. When he finished he nodded.

"Been thinking about that man's face. I'm not sure now who it is, but I've got an idea you can look into. He's tall, maybe six feet or so. Little on the skinny side. Wore a blue shirt, blue jeans, and had that dumb kid's backpack on."

"What color was the backpack, Mr. Bascomb?"

"Color? Thought I told you. It was mostly black."

"You said you thought you recognized him. Who do you think the man might be?"

"Well, now, I don't aim to get nobody in trouble. You know if I said I think it was one man and it wasn't him at all that could be bad."

"That's a chance we have to take, Mr. Bascomb," Chief Sanderson said. "You give us a name and we'll make sure that we don't hurt or embarrass anyone if he isn't the right man. Like, if he was in Portland for three days, or had an air tight alibi."

"Oh, yeah. Right. I know about alibis. I watch a lot of detective shows on the TV. You ever seen

Crime Stoppers? Great show. I watch it every Friday night."

"Mr. Bascomb," Hardy said. "I've seen that one. Who do you think the man you saw was? Somebody here in town?"

"Oh, yes. Now I'm not positive but sure looked like the man who owns the grocery store, Broderson. Yeah, King Broderson."

"That's good, Mr. Bascomb," the Chief said. "Do you think of any other men in town it might have been? We can check out two or three if you can give us any more names."

"Nope. That's about it. More I think on it, the more I can see that one face of the man we usually see when we buy groceries on Sunday afternoons."

Chief Sanderson nodded. "Good. We understand. We'll be sure that no one but us know about your seeing this man. It could be dangerous for you. Don't tell anyone else what you saw. All right?"

"Oh, damn. Never thought of that. On the screen witnesses to killings are always in danger. Yes. I'll keep mum about this. Hope I have helped."

They said goodbye, thanked him again, and went downstairs. Chief Sanderson talked to the store owner.

"How is your father doing?"

"He's making out pretty good. We go on lots of outings in my ramp van where his wheelchair can roll right in and lock in place in the passenger side front seat space."

"How old is he now?"

"Eighty-two."

"His mind is it sharp? Could he have seen this man across the street?"

"Oh, yes. He's good. Doesn't fantasize or go off telling wild stories. And he has a pair of big binoculars he's always using."

"Mr. Bascomb, it might be a good idea if you kept this confidential. Don't tell anyone we were here or what your father saw."

"Oh, yes. I see. Could be dangerous if the real killer found out about Dad."

"Right. Thanks for your help." They said good bye and went outside.

"What do you think about King Broderson?" Hardy asked the Chief.

"Doesn't sound right. He did have it right about the black backpack. But I've never seen King Broderson wear a pair of blue jeans. Besides, he's no more than five ten and far from slender. Still we'll check it out with King. Now might be a good time."

"How can we do that without making him ask where he was last night about five?"

"First we try to see if he has an alibi without any tie in with any crime."

"Sounds tough. Mind if I tag along with you?"

"Not a chance. I'm going to ask him about something to do with the Barbershop Ballad contest. It will look like just a normal question. You can wait in your car."

Five minutes later, Chief Sanderson went into the Broderson Grocery and looked around. He didn't see King. At the counter, he asked if he could talk to King for a minute.

The checkout girl, a twenty-something with real red hair in a long pigtail down her back, shook her head.

"No way, Chief. He and his wife went on a trip to

Hawaii three days ago. Going to be gone a week. He's been working too hard on the new shopping center and his doctor told him to get away."

"Oh, then I guess I can't find out what I wanted to know about the Barbershop contest. I'll see him when he gets back."

Hardy had been pacing outside the grocery. When the Chief came out he pounced.

"So?"

"Ben saw someone, we know that. Probably it was the killer. That black backpack ties it up neatly. Only the man wasn't King Broderson. He and his wife left for Hawaii three days ago."

Hardy nodded. "Damn. I was afraid it might be something like that. Otherwise it would have been too simple to nail this guy. So just what the hell do we do now?"

"One idea. It's a long shot. Remember how that serial killer in New York City was caught after he got a parking ticket? Son of Sam I think it was. Why don't you check with the other guys and see if anybody wrote a ticket within three blocks of Dr. Warnick's place last night. We might get lucky."

"Yeah a real long shot. I didn't write any tickets yesterday. I'll check with Bob and Al."

Back in his patrol car, Hardy called Bob Young who was on duty.

"Tickets yesterday? Yep, two. One for speeding down Pacific Highway and the other one for overtime parking."

"The parking one, was it anywhere near Dr. Warnick's office?"

"Oh, yeah, I see where you're going. Nope it was

over near the college. No help there. I think Al did some tickets yesterday."

"I'll call him. Hope he's home. Thanks."

Al Turley came on the phone after the first ring.

"Yeah, I'm here."

"Al, Hardy. You write any tickets yesterday for a car anywhere near Dr. Warnick's office?"

"Damned if I didn't. Actually about a block away. Some old brown clunker had outdated plates on it."

"Great. You have your ticket book with you?"

"Nope, at the station. But I put a copy in my shift ending report as usual."

"It's a long shot, but it just might tie in somehow. What kind of a car?"

"Hard to tell. It had been repaired and repainted, and customized, but it looked like a basic Chevrolet from eighty eight or eighty nine."

"That was the make and year of the car that picked up Willy when this all started. I'm gonna go down and check. Run that old plate and see what we get."

"Let me know if I solved four murders."

"Will do. Take care."

The night officer on duty manned the phone from eight to midnight, then turned on the answering machine and went on his normal patrol.

On his short drive back to the station, Hardy called and asked Officer Doug Olson to look up the copy of the ticket. He had it when Hardy hurried in the front door.

"Got it," Olson said. "The time on it is for a little after five thirty p.m."

"Let's run the plate."

One phone call later they had it.

"Shows last registered owner as a Pat Brown, in Tigard. A note that says the car was totaled over a year ago."

"Damn, no help," Olson said.

"Might be at that. Al said it was an old beat up and reworked Chevy, maybe an eighty nine. That's also the make and near year of the beat up old Chevy that was used to pick up Willy Haskins, our first victim."

"Not much."

"But it could be another strand of circumstantial evidence if we go to trial on this guy without any eye witness or much solid evidence. I'll tell the Chief what we found. He won't be thrilled but it's another nail for the coffin lid."

"But wasn't that Willy pick up Chevy loaded with five or six different colors of paint?" Olson asked.

"Yep, but a spray can and a quart of brown paint could turn it into a brown clunker."

Hardy checked his email. He had two messages. One from the Sheriff's forensic squad. "Removed the .22 caliber slug from the wood. It is deformed but not so much that I got some good lines and grooves from it. Putting it in the evidence file on the Gomez case."

He printed out two copies and showed it to Olson.

"Another thread of evidence? Now all we need is the gun that fired it."

Hardy deleted the other email offering him male enhancement with a simple pill, and headed home. Nothing else he could do tonight.

ED HAD WORKED HARD MOST of the day. He and Uriah had settled on three new name brands of furniture to feature in the new store, and were in the process of selecting the pieces they wanted on the floor. Some would be in stock but most on special order.

Uriah came in about six.

"We did good work today, Mr. Rathwood."

"Yes we did Uriah. Was there something?"

"You did get a call about ten minutes ago. It was a friend in Hillsboro who said he had an eight o'clock special for you. I took his number and said you would return his call." He handed Ed a piece of paper with a phone number.

When Uriah left, Ed grinned. He was on a roll. A special meant she would be one selected especially for him and thirteen. He grinned again and reached for the phone. Yes, he was on a roll and it was getting better and better.

28

THE NEXT MORNING, Chief Sanderson kept the night man on duty and talked to all four of his officers. He was as near to panic as Hardy had ever seen him.

"We've got to stop this slaughter. But I don't know how in hell we can. We're getting evidence, but it's no good without a suspect to test it with. The night of Doc Warnick's death a man said he saw someone wearing a black backpack knock on the Doc's door. He said he knew who it was but he was wrong. The man he named has been out of town for three days."

"Chief, I've been thinking about that," Hardy said. "The witness said he thought it was a man who they saw every Sunday when they bought groceries. Are there any men working at the grocery store who might fit the description?"

"Good, Hardy. Might be productive. You check that out this morning. Any other ideas how we can dig out this killer?"

"The old car I ticketed might be a lead," Al Turley

said. "So now we watch for this twenty-year-old brown clunker Chevy."

"Yeah, that's good. Only thing is if I was the killer and used that rig, I'd hide it in a garage somewhere so nobody could see it. Then I'd paint it horse black. Still, we watch for it wherever we are."

Bob Long shook his h head. "I've got nothing. I've been trying to establish a pattern. The only pattern is that there isn't any pattern. Looks like he's deliberately mixing up his victims. First a boy, then a young girl, then a man and now a woman. It leaves me nothing to use any logic on. I'd like to get some idea who he might target next. But I'm stymied."

"Hardy, you ever finish checking on those nine names on that kitty litter list?"

"Damn, no. So much else has been going on I just mislaid the list. I did think of one way to cut it down. We know at least three of the names. None of those three fit the description we have. One guy is in his seventies, another one is so fat he can hardly walk, and the third one is not over five feet three inches tall."

"So you still have six to check." Chief Sanderson said. Get it done today."

"Yes sir."

"Olson, you have any ideas?"

"I was thinking about putting two squad cars out on patrol,"

"Might," the Chief said. "Only none of the kills took place during the day." The Chief looked at his officers. "Okay, that's about it. We need to get some results. We need somebody in custody. Make a special push. Thanks."

The four men scattered.

Hardy dug out his list of suspects on the kitty litter project. First he changed into civilian clothes. Better for a see and talk job like this. The uniform sometimes made people freeze up.

First he went to the Broderson Grocery. He knew one of the clerks there. He found her stocking shelves.

"Hey Beth, how's it going?"

"Good. I'm going to go to junior college."

"Outstanding. Hey, I have a friend who is looking for a part time job. Any chance King has a need for more help?"

"Lordy no. I keep telling him he's got too many of us here now."

"Who all works here?" Hardy asked.

"Us three girls, and Chance, who is fairly new. He's an older guy in his fifties, but sharp. Then we have Lonny our meat man. He's a little weird but nice. He's about forty five or so. That's us. Course when the new store opens we'll need at least ten more people."

"Thanks, I'll tell him to get on the waiting list. You take care now."

Hardy went outside and kicked the front tire on his Ford. That was a blowout. Now who did he have on that cat litter list?

Strange name. Uriah. Uriah Condit. He'd never heard the name before except for that British rock star. The address was listed as 302 Third Avenue. He pulled up and decided on the survey ploy. He rang the bell on a modest home on a good street. A woman in her forties answered the door.

"Good morning I'm taking a quick survey about cat food. What brad do you usually buy?"

"That's strange. Cat food. We don't own a cat so I'm afraid I can't help you."

"Yes, that is strange. You were on my list of names of cat owners. Must have been a mix up. Maybe your husband has a cat he hasn't told you about."

She laughed. "Afraid not. Uriah doesn't like cats. We used to have a dog, but she died of old age. You have a good day now." The door closed.

Hardy went back to his Ford and looked at the next name. No one was home at two of the places. The next one was a woman in her sixties who said her husband was in a wheel chair and couldn't come to the door. Yes, they had an inside cat and used PussyFoot litter. He thanked her and left.

His fifth call was more productive. The man answering the door was tall, slight and in his thirties. He said yes, he bought PussyFoot litter because it killed the smell better than any other.

"That's what we like to hear," Hardy said. "Thanks for your input."

"That's it?" the man asked.

"Just a simple one question survey," Hardy said. He thanked the man again and left. In his car he put a star by the man's name. He could bear watching.

His final call turned out to be to a woman in her twenties. She said her husband wasn't home. He was serving his second tour as a Marine in Germany. She expected him back in two more months.

So much for the list. Back at the station Olson looked at the list and grinned when Hardy said that Bill Jackson could be a suspect.

"Not a high percentage bet," Olson said. "Reentered Bill is the pastor at our Baptist Church."

"Great, you just shot me down. Now all I have are two call backs." Hardy told the Chief that there was no good suspects working at Broderson's Grocery and that no good ones on the litter list. But he had two not at home names to work yet.

The Chief grunted. "Figures. Sit down, we need to talk. You were being careful about your routine, so you vary it?"

"Working at it, Chief. Sometimes I forget. Old habits…"

"Next time you forget you could be dead. Don't forget. Do you have a hid out?"

"Hide out? You mean a second weapon, like in mid back holster? Nope. Never thought I needed one."

"Now you do." The Chief took a plastic wrapped package from his bottom desk drawer. "Open it."

Hardy took the plastic away and inside he found a .38 revolver with a two inch barrel in an ankle holster.

"That's mine. I wore it for years in Portland. Decided I didn't need it out here. Now you do need it, so it's yours until this emergency is over and our killer is either dead or behind bars."

"Honest, Chief. I really don't think…"

Sanderson cut him off with a wave of his hand.

"Doesn't matter what you think about this. I'm giving you an order to wear this at all times, unless you're sleeping or swimming. You understand?"

Hardy frowned then lifted his brows. "Yeah, I guess. Sure. Gonna take some getting used to."

"One day and you won't even know it's there. Now get out of here and go catch me a killer. Put that strap around your ankle first. Here, I'll show you the best way to do it."

29

A PHONE CALL interrupted the ankle holster fitting. Chief Sanderson took the call. He put on the phone's speaker.

"Yeah, so?"

"Philbin with forensics. We finished our go round on that backpack. Some interesting stuff. We found the killer's prints all over the chloroform bottle. Matched the others. No surprise there. The morphine ampoules were the same as used on the body and had the same lot number on them.

"The sticky tape was generic. Can be bought in dozens of stores almost anywhere. We found a black baseball style cap. There are black hairs in it that we are running for DNA but almost for certain they will match the DNA we have on him from the other evidence.

"Also a pair of those plastic riot cuffs like you guys use. Don't know where he got them and they are hard to find. If we could find out who sold them it could help."

"Yeah, we'll do some checking," the Chief said.

"So next we found a small note pad that had an address on it. We're not sure who it belongs to."

"What is it?" The Chief asked. "We can chase it down and see who it belongs to."

"Yes, that would be a help. The address is written down as 255 Fifth Avenue."

Hardy jumped up from where he had been sitting. "You're kidding, right? That's my address."

"You damn sure of that address, Philbin? That isn't an address you had on your desk or something?"

"Nope. We inventoried the bag as soon as we got it and the pad and address are on the original list. That's all we found."

"Yeah, yeah. Okay. I believe you. So now we have a real problem. Thanks for the input."

The Chief hung up and jolted out of his chair. "Jones, you know what this means? He has you on his sign board for some reason. Maybe he just doesn't like you because of the newspaper piece. Most likely you could be his next victim."

The Chief paced around his office. "So, that means that you, Jones and your wife, are on a paid vacation. You're going out of state somewhere until we nail this bastard to the wall. I want you gone from here tomorrow. It's too big a risk to let you stay in town. Get out of the state somewhere."

Hardy Jones was still standing. He stared eye to eye with the Chief.

"Sorry, but I can't do that. I'd never be able to live with myself. I'd be running away from a fight. I won't do that, Chief."

"I'm giving you a direct order. If you disobey it, I can fire you."

"Right, you can. But that wouldn't do any good, because I'd still stay around town trying to find this killer."

The Chief groaned and sat down at his desk. "Why does this damn job have to be so difficult?" He shook his head. "Figured you'd say something like that. So I go to plan B."

"Didn't know you had a plan B, Chief."

"Oh, I do. I hire a new man, a security guard or some such. I'll put him in our uniform, give him a gun and he will be your constant companion. He will be with you twenty four hours a day. You have a two bedroom house so he sleeps there. No arguments, that's the way it has to be. There's a security guard outfit in Hillsboro run by an ex-cop. He should have an ex-cop who can fit our need. Now let's get that hideout strapped on. Oh, yeah. I've got a box of shells for you. Want you to hit the range and put about twenty five rounds through that .38. It handles different from your Glock."

"So this guy is going to babysit me? No way I can get out of it?"

"Not a chance. Now get out of here and test fire that .38 of mine."

ED RATHWOOD HAD BEEN at the store a half hour before it opened and before Uriah arrived. He signed some checks, got a deposit ready to take to the bank, and generally cleaned up his desk. Today he wore a pair of sun tan pants, an outside brown shirt and picked up a backpack. It was a brown one. He knew he had a black one somewhere. Just where he didn't know.

A shiver went down his spine. The black one was the one he always used on his strike missions. He had it at the Gomez house he was sure. Did he leave it there? He shivered then regained his composure. There was nothing in it that could tie it to him. He was still in the clear.

Uriah came up the steps with some papers about the new store.

"Just put them on my desk, Uriah. I'm getting bored around here. I need some exercise, so I'm off on a bike ride—fifteen or twenty miles sounds about right. See you when I get back."

Uriah was used to his boss's sometimes strange behavior. He took it in stride and went back to his own desk to get ready for the day.

Ed wore a brown baseball cap and sun glasses. He pedaled first past Professor Dr. Clarence P. Rider's house not far from the downtown campus of the university. The professor's blue Buick was still in the driveway. He had only a half hour to get to his first class at nine o'clock.

Ed turned back to the camps and followed several students walking and riding bikes toward the college. In is outfit he looked a lot like the others. No one would remember him. He parked and locked his bike in a rack outside the music building and wandered in. Dr. Rider's first class today was music history on the second floor in room 203.

Ed climbed the steps and found the room. As the room began to fill up, Ed walked in and sat down in a chair near the back. He watched the kids come in until there were only three seats left. Dr. Rider arrived ten minutes before class was set to begin. He chatted with students, answered questions, and seemed to enjoy himself.

Yes, definitely an over achiever trying to spread his knowledge and experience to the students. Just before the class started, Ed slipped out the door without the professor seeing him go.

Ed went back to his bike. The man was precise, punctual, and functioned on a routine that probably did not vary more than a few minutes day in and day out. This class was over at eleven and the scholar would go for his lunch.

Ed wheeled his bike out into the street, began a ride that would take him out of town, and toward Hillsboro on back roads. He'd go out for forty five minutes then ride back. It was always slower coming back.

This was a bike route he had ridden many times before when the pressures built up he needed the exercise to help dampen them down and hopefully squelch them completely.

At his turn around spot he pulled under a big maple tree, opened his backpack, and took out a can of Coke he had packed in ice before he left the office. It helped give him a sugar surge for the return trip.

As he rode, he planned just how he would do in the good professor. There was no rush, but he figured next week sometime.

Back at the camps, Ed spotted Dr. Rider's blue Buick in its reserved spot in the faculty parking lot. The music professor stepped into the Buick precisely at eleven fifteen. He would drive home where his wife would fix his lunch. His next class today wasn't until two thirty and Ed guessed that Rider took a small nap after his lunch.

On Tuesday's he had one more class and then meetings until nearly six o'clock with other faculty members in his department. He was head of the department so had a lot of other things to worry about besides teaching Ed figured. Dr. Rider would get home about seven for a late dinner then he'd watch TV or listen to classical music until his usual bed time of ten thirty.

Ed had a quick lunch himself at the Burger Bar then followed the professor back to his second class of the day. It was a routine he had set and followed precisely.

Ed pedaled his bike back to the store. Checked with Uriah to see if there were any emergencies. There weren't so he decided to go home to change clothes. Tonight he felt like a good dinner. He'd drive into Portland to a favorite sea food restaurant and see if the Maine lobster were in yet. Tomorrow would be the day. He would set the date, time and place for his fatal, final meeting with Dr. Clarence P. Rider. Before he got out the door, the phone rang.

"Hey buddy. Thought I missed you." It was King Broderson.

"Got a big flap that we've got to take care of tonight. Calling a special meeting at the library at seven thirty. Hope you van be there."

"Damnit, King. I was half way to Portland for a lobster dinner."

"Uriah said you were still in the store."

"Yeah, I am. I was wishing lobster. I'll be there." Ed groaned. He'd have to settle for one of the poorly cooked steak at the Glen Café.

. . .

PROMPTLY AT SEVEN THIRTY, King Broderson opened the meeting. He drove right to the problem.

"Well, now we've done it. We're so popular this year that I'm told we have a lot more entries than ever before and some are afraid we won't be able to narrow down all the entrants to the finals on Sunday night. Dr. Rider, this falls on your shoulders. What have you heard and how can we cope?"

Dr. Rider stood. He still wore his blue suit that he had on for his classes. He nodded.

"Yes, King, I was told about the mounting number of entrants and I have a plan that will let us get the work done. We will cut off entrants at thirty-two which is about twenty more than last year. But we will eliminate the quartets with a new system. They will be divided into eight groups of four. They will compete against each other. The two top quartets move on to the semifinals. Those eight contests will leave us with sixteen quartets.

Eight winners in each bracket will be divided into four which will compete producing four semifinalists. Then the four semis will compete Sunday night. That leaves us two finalists. I figure we can get the first two rounds done on Friday night and Saturday. Then Sunday morning we have the semis, with the finals as usual Sunday night. We may have to cut down the length of each quartet's performance. We're working on that." He paused and looked around.

"Oh we will seed the top ten contestants like they do in tennis, so the top quartets do not go against each other in the first round."

King nodded. "Sounds like it should work. Anyone have any objections or suggestions?"

He looked over the eight members who had made the meeting. Nobody said a word.

"Okay, then, looks like our little crisis is over and solved and we're back on track with no other changes needed. This meeting is adjourned. Remember, we have only two weeks until show time."

The meeting broke up. Ed watched the music man. He was trim and looked fit. He was maybe sixty, gray hair, a six hundred dollar suit and an old school tie from the Ivy League. Ed let a secret little grin shape his face. The professor would not be around when the quartets started to sing.

30

WHEN ED GOT HOME that night from the Barbershop Ballad meeting, his mother met him in the living room.

"Sit down, Ed, we have to talk."

Ed grinned. "The last time you said that you gave me a dozen condoms and showed me how to use then."

"I hope that you always do. No, this is slightly more important. I think that it's time that you know something more about me than you do now."

"Hey, I know that you came from old money in Portland and still swirl around in the social set in there every now and then."

"Do you have any idea how much I'm worth?"

"Not the slightest, Mother. I'm making money on the store now. Arranged my own financing for the new store and I'm rolling along just fine."

"When I was your age I was pure hell on roller skates. I had money. I had position. I fucked any good looking man I wanted to and they asked for more. After about a year, word got back to my straight laced father and he sent me to Switzerland for two years.

"Didn't change much. I picked up German quickly and I went right on whoring around. It all ended when one of the gents got too rough and I stabbed him with a sharp letter opener. It drove into his heart and he died in seconds. It was his apartment, so I got my things, wiped off any prints I might have left, and took a plane home the next day. Yes, we did have airliners back then."

"So you killed him and ran. You did a bad thing, Mother. But I'm not surprised. You sometimes show streaks of abject cruelty."

"You mean the dogs? I really hate dogs, all dogs. Puppies are okay for a month or two, but then they grow up and turn into dogs." She laughed. "Remember that one we killed out at the lake? I'd had lots of practice before then. For a while I'd dog nap any dog I could find, kill them any number of ways, and then bury them out in the brush in our outback."

"Why are you telling me this, Mother?"

"Because I want you to stop."

"Stop what, Mother."

"You know damn well what. They are going to catch you and I don't want you to spend the rest of your life in prison."

"I'm not sure what you're saying, Mother. If you think I've done something, come out with it."

Elmira Rathwood turned away. "Getting back to the money. I just had an audit and a compilation of all of my holdings. Roughly speaking Rathwood Inc. is worth a little over twenty five million dollars. Think what you could do with that kind of money. What I am suggesting is that you give the store to Uriah, he's earned it. Then tomorrow I want you to fly out to the south of France. Don't worry about extradition. I've got a complete history for you including a new name, social security card, driver's license, and three bank cards with over five hundred thousand in each of the accounts."

Ed broke up laughing. "I don't believe what I just heard. Why in the world would I want to leave town and the business? I don't care about your millions. I'm getting on well by myself."

"Edward. Don't play games. I know about the four people here in town who you have killed."

He stared hard at her, his face shifting from his laugh to a stern frown.

"You don't need to deny it. I've seen your private little collection in the room over the garage. Do you think I'm blind or just stupid?"

"Mother, dearest. You're doing all this just for me?"

"Absolutely not. I'm doing it for me. What standing do you think I'd have in Portland social circles if my son was convicted as a mass murderer? I'd not be welcome at any of the functions. My own little charities here in town would be ignored. No, my one and only son, I'm not doing it for you. Not at all. I'm doing it for me."

"You think they are close to catching me, charging me with the killings?"

"Not really sure how close. But you've been making mistakes and leaving clues. How do I know? I'm close friends with Abigail Sanderson, the Chief of Police's wife. We get together regularly to play bridge. The Chief is a talker and he talks too much. I know of several clues they have. For instance they have your DNA and about that old rattletrap of a Chevy you have out in the shed. They don't know the DNA is yours or that the car is yours, but they might down the line."

"How did they..."

"He didn't say. But believe me, they have that and more. It's time you went on a vacation with your new name. How about tomorrow?"

"Mother, I haven't admitted that I did anything."

"You don't have to. I've seen Willy's letterman warm up jacket. And the other things. I don't care if you admit it or not. I'm trying to save your life here. You have to get out while you can, before any suspicion points to you. Once it does, you won't be able to travel as far away as Hillsboro."

"Have you killed anyone else, Mother? I mean lately?"

"Certainly not."

"What about Juanita, that illegal Mexican maid we had for a while. You always got mad at her. I've seen you beat her with your fists when you were really crazy furious with her."

"We don't talk about Juanita. She quit and went back to Mexico."

"Or your anger got a little out of hand one day and you had to dig a really big hole out in the brush. I bet it took you all day."

Elmira jumped up and paced around the large room. "I certainly did no such thing. Monstrous of you to even suggest it."

"Then why are you so worked up? Hey a little tit for tat here. You accuse me of killing four people. I only accused you of killing one in a fit of anger."

Elmira stopped pacing. She sat in the chair opposite Ed. "Let's not talk about that any more. What it comes down to is that you will soon be in danger and I won't be. So, will you go to France or England or Switzerland?"

Ed leaned back on the couch and laced his fingers together under his head. "Always wanted to see France. But I'd need to be well situated, say five million in a bank over there." He looked at her. She always had been close with money and never talked about it. He waited. She stared at him.

"Yes, that would be easy. Getting you set up with the new name and background was the hard part. I had to go to San Francisco to get the last of the documents including a birth certificate and the Social Security card. Those people charge outrageous rates. Now I have everything and the money is in three banks in Portland. It can be easily transferred once you get set up in Europe."

"I appreciate all of your hard work."

"Then you'll go this week?"

"Afraid not. I have two more projects."

"They will catch you for sure."

"I'll know if they are even sniffing at me. Trust me on this one, Mother. I'm the one with the experience."

"I'll take care of the store. It's still in my name, you know. And yes, I do have a will. You inherit it all, but it won't do you any good if you're rotting in jail, or if they kill you first."

He stood and walked around the room. When he came back he grinned. "Mother, I like your plan. But first these two situations. Then it's off to the pretty girls in Southern France."

31

THAT SAME AFTERNOON Hardy checked on his last two PussyFoot users. He wanted to get that out of the way before his baby sitter arrived. The first place he called was an apartment house where they allowed cats. The woman was in her eighties and said yes, she used PussyFoot. He thanked her quickly and moved on to the next address.

It was an older house and he could smell the cat urine as soon as the door opened. The man who answered the door was in his forties, bald, and with a limp.

"Hell no, don't use that damn PussyFoot no more. Too expensive. We go through it in a week. We got six cats. They bitching because I stopped buying?"

"Just a routine check, sir. Nothing to worry about."

From there he went to the only shop in town he knew of that might have the plastic riot cuffs. It was a small place that had costumes, party favors, decorations, and gifts.

"Oh no, we never stock those," a woman in her

fifties said. She was overweight and had a wild hair do that looked like the sixties. "Teenagers like them and that gets them in trouble. We stopped stocking them a year ago."

Hardy thanked her and drove to Hillsboro, seven miles down Pacific Highway. He knew of one joke shop there that might have them. They had all sorts of jokes, signs, books, and costumes. The man who came out of the back room was in his twenties with bleached blonde hair in spikes. He grinned at Hardy's question.

"Hey man, you got some chick you want to tie up a little, right? Sure, we have them. Don't sell a lot but now and then."

"You remember a man in his thirties, about six two who bought some recently?"

"Oh, yeah. I sold three pair to a guy like him a couple of months ago. I really dug him, but he didn't seem interested when I gave him the signals. You know to have a good time. I guess he was straight."

"If I had a picture, could you identify him?"

"Hell yes. He was a rah rah kind of goy."

"Did you get a name and address?"

"Oh no. Our sales are all anonymous we don't want to get anyone in trouble."

"All right. If we get a picture, I'll be back to see you."

"You a cop, right? Even if you're not in uniform. This guy do something bad?"

"He did. I'll get back to you."

Hardy drove to the station and wrote out his report on the two missions. Then he went out on a fender bender the other side of the college. He wrapped it up quickly with an exchange of names and told them they didn't have to file an accident report.

ED CHECKED his new building out at the shopping center. They had some of the framing up. It would be a two story affair, with lots and lots of display space. That's when he realized if it all worked out he wouldn't be here to see the place finished. The South of France. Yeah.

The professor. He realized that he couldn't do the man at home. His wife would be there. Which meant it had to be in his car driving home or at the college. He chose the college. Two days ago he had gone to watch the professor and found his routine had changed. Now he was staying later at school. Evidently he had dinner early and went back to his office. Ed knew he had to check on him tonight to see how late he stayed, what he did during the late hours, and how it would affect his plans.

That evening he put on a pair of blue jeans, a Superman tee shirt, and a baseball cap from the NY Yankees, and his shades. He bicycled over to the college. Lights were on in the several rooms the professor used.

Ed parked, locked his bike, hoisted his backpack on one shoulder, and climbed to the second floor where the professor's office was situated. Two students sat on chairs in the hall outside the office. One looked up and shook his head. His hair hung around his shoulders and he had a full beard. His clothes were pure college: Bermuda shorts and a tee shirt.

"The old prof is running late on his appointments. You might as well sit down."

"How late?" Ed asked.

"At least a half hour. But I got to see him to work on my thesis subject."

"How late does he stay?" Ed asked.

"His last appointment is at eight thirty, so he's out of here about nine." The kid shook his head. "Don't know why he stays so late. Hey, you new to the department?"

"Trying to transfer in."

"Good luck, took me almost a year."

"Yeah. I'll come back later." Ed turned and walked down the hall to the stairs. That was a little dangerous talking to that kid for so long. But the musician wouldn't be able to ID him. Not with his sunglasses on and his cap. He picked up his bike and rode toward home thinking about what supplies he would need for his date with the professor tomorrow night.

He was a long block from his home when the Forest Glen Fire Department's tanker truck raced past him. To his surprise it wheeled into the entrance to the Rathwood estate. He pedaled faster then, saw the truck stopped in front of the house, and his mother pointing to the west.

Then he saw the smoke. It came not from the house but behind it. What could be burning back there? All that was back there was the shack with his old car inside.

No, no it couldn't be his Chevy. He'd had it since he was a teenager. He raced in the entrance and followed the fire truck around the house on a lane that led to the old shack.

Yes it was on fire. The whole damn thing was one mass of flames. No chance to save his car. He knew at once what had happened. His dear, sweet, mother had set it on fire then waited long enough for the car to be a total cinder and twisted metal before she called the firemen.

The volunteers did a good job, knocking down the flames in the weeds, leaves and brush around the shack, but there was nothing they could do on the shack itself.

Ed knew all five of the firemen who had responded. He talked to Wally, who was wetting down the brush around the shack.

"Too far gone to save the building," he told Ed. "Sorry about that. But we can stop the woods back here from burning."

They had one two inch hose spraying on the shack itself to cool off the flames but there was no chance to put them out.

A half hour later the shack was a forest of half burned two by fours, roof rafters, and the remains of the old Chevy, twisted, caved in, and party melted by the intensity of the fire.

The firemen made one last survey of the ashes, put out a few hot spots, then rolled in their hoses and drove away.

Ed had recognized Hardy Jones, the cop. He was one of the fire fighters. Ed made a point of not talking to him. Ed had not seen his mother anywhere near the fire. As he poked through the still hot ashes, she came out showing a sly grin.

He was too angry with her to be civil.

"You didn't have to be fucking burning up my car. I

told you they would never find it and if they did it wasn't really evidence."

"Me? I didn't do a thing. Must have been some oily rags or maybe a chipmunk knocked over a can of gasoline. Happens."

"Don't lie to me, Mother. I told you that I'm going to go to France. Now let me finish my work,"

"It's for your own good, Edward. Now, we won't speak about it again. It's done and over with. I want you to concentrate on your work and not make any blunders this late in the game."

Ed laughed. "Old girl, you are one tough bitch. You have more guts than brains. But it seems to work for you. Twenty five million. I should have asked for ten."

"You've got the ten. Now be good and don't make any mistakes. I've got a drink waiting for you in the living room. Let's get out of this smoke and smell."

Ed took a deep breath. So the car was gone. He had ten million. He'd just earned five more. The car wasn't worth nearly that much.

"Yes, Mother, I think I can use that drink."

32

THE NEXT MORNING Hardy met his baby sitter and body guard. He was in his forties, had retired from the Portland police department, and had been working as an armed guard on a Brinks money truck. His name was Fred Newton, about six feet tall and solid at maybe two hundred pounds, Hardy figured. He liked the man's friendly grin. His hair was black and thinning on top and he wore glasses for reading. He had on a Forest Glen Police uniform. It was a little large for him but he said his wife could fix it up fine. He looked like a cop.

"Hi, I'm the guy you're babysitting," Hardy said.

"We call it body guarding", Fred said. "I won't get in your way but I'll have your back seven twenty four."

"Yeah, that's what I hear. The Chief had the side windows on one of the patrol cars shaded down with one way tinting so you can see out, but nobody can see in. That way you can ride in the back seat without anyone knowing you're there."

"Good idea but let's put inside handles back on the two doors so I can get out in a rush if I have to."

"Right. Hadn't thought of that. We can pick up some at the Ford dealer. Understand you did time with the Portland PD."

"Yeah. Twenty two years and three months. Time to move on. Any chance I could get on full time here?"

"Not my call, Fred. We sure cold use the help. Best to talk to the Chief about that." Hardy's phone rang. It was the front desk.

"First run of the day," Hardy said. He listened to the phone. "Yes, on Pacific Glen Way. A two car crash with injuries. On our way."

"Let's roll, Fred. Nasty wreck."

By the time they arrived, the two drivers were in an argument. Hardy separated them then looked at the injured man sitting on the lawn. He kept moaning about his legs. Hardy took a quick check and figured one or both were broken. The cars had hit head on and the larger one smashed the Honda into a heap of metal.

It was twenty minutes before the ambulance arrived from Hillsboro. They would take the injured man to the hospital there.

Hardy called for a tow truck. That took another twenty minutes. It pulled the two wrecks apart and towed one away. It would be back for the other one. Hardy got the two drivers to trade names, phone numbers, and insurance companies.

"Yes, ma'am that's right. You'll need to go to the Police Station and fill out an accident report." He looked at the older man who had driven the Honda. "You'll have to file a report as well, sir. Do it today."

Back in the patrol car, Hardy looked at Fred in the back seat. "So, Fred, that's the kind of cop work we do the most of here in Forest Glen. Not as glamorous as the big city, but it gets the job done."

It went that way for the rest of the day. Fred stayed in the back seat and watched for anyone following them. He thought an old blue pickup was tailing them, but it turned off after two blocks and Fred didn't see it again. They had lunch at the Forest Glen Café and then did patrol for the rest of the shift.

At the station Fred grinned.

"Not bad at all. Feels good to be back in uniform and to have a Glock in my holster. What's our shift for tomorrow?"

"We do the four to midnight, so bring along our night vision. The Chief expects trouble, but I don't. You driving back to Hillsboro?"

"Yeah, fifteen minutes. See you tomorrow about four."

IT WAS seven thirty that same night and for Ed Rathwood, it was kill time. He helped Uriah close up the store and waved out the door. Then he went upstairs and put on his student outfit, complete with a Stones tee shirt, black cap, and tan pants. He put in his brown backpack what he would need. At the last moment he decided to leave a message. He picked up a piece of letter sized paper off his desk, a marker pen, and wrote on it in large letters: OVERACHIEVER.

He slipped it unfolded into his backpack and checked what he had inside. Yes, everything he would need. He'd be damn sure not to leave it at the site this time. He took with him two pair of pliers, a pair of side cutters, sticky tape, riot cuffs, a spare tee shirt, a folded hand towel, and two knives. One had a six inch blade that was thin and only a half inch wide. The other one was a hunting knife that he kept razor sharp. Yes, all he would need.

He waited until eight thirty then spent five minutes riding his bike to the music building at the university. He parked it in the rack and put on a lock like the others used. Then he walked up to the second floor and looked down the hall. Nobody sat in the waiting chair outside of Dr. Rider's door. He stood in an alcove at the far end of the hall. Anyone coming out of that office probably would go the short way to get to the stairs.

Ten minutes later he heard the door open, some laughter, and then the door closed. A girl in gray slacks and a white blouse came out and went the other way down the hall.

Ed moved. He ran lightly to the target door and tried the knob. It was unlocked. He pushed it open and stepped into the office. It was twice as big as he had expected. Dr. Rider looked up from where he stood behind a large desk covered with papers, folders, and music scores.

"Sorry appointment time is over for today. Come back tomorrow."

"Dr. Driver, I'm afraid that won't do. I have to talk to you right now."

"I don't place you. Are you in one of my classes?"

"Didn't think you would remember me." Ed walked up to the side of the desk.

"Now see here. You need to get an appointment. Talk to my secretary tomorrow. I'm ready to go home."

"You can stay for a while longer, professor."

Ed jumped around the desk and caught the musician from the back with a strangle hold around his neck.

"Now just relax, professor and this won't hurt so much." Ed rammed the sixty year old down into his desk chair. He grabbed the sticky tape from his back pack and tore off two pieces which he pressed firmly over the musician's mouth.

"Now you won't have to talk." Ed took out the riot cuffs, stood up the professor, pulled his hands behind his back, and cinched them up tight with the plastic binders. He pushed him back down into the chair.

"Now we're getting somewhere, Dr. Rider. Oh, where do you keep that favorite violin of yours? I hear you were pretty good in your younger years."

Ed used a second pair of cuffs to cinch the professor's ankles together then began his search. He found a violin in a cabinet near the far wall laid out on a black velvet cloth.

"There it is." He took out the instrument, found the side cutter pliers in his backpack, and cut the strings from the violin.

He watched the horror on the musician's face as he saw his prize violin being violated.

"Don't worry about the strings, Dr. Rider. You won't be needing them anymore." As he talked, Ed took a pair of pliers and twisted the ends of the strings together until he had a line about four feet long.

"Interesting, no, Dr. Rider?" He watched sweat bead on the musician's face and run down across the tape. "I see you are concerned. Good, I want you to worry a little. Now where are the rest of those instruments that must be here?"

Ed found what he looked for in an adjoining room.

It was half filled with musical instruments. He carried out a huge string base, then a dozen other instruments from saxophones to trumpets and oboes, violins, and tubas.

Dr. Rider watched all of this with eyes that were wild and darting from side to side. He tried to yell from time to time, but the sound couldn't get past his lips. At last he sagged in the chair.

Ed showed him the length of violin string wire.

"You know a lot more about these strings than I do. I see some of them are steel, some have synthetic cores which give deeper and more satisfying tones." Ed laughed. "You know all this, but it won't matter. I've twisted and tied them together to form a strong long violin string. I bet you can't guess what I'm going to do with it." Ed looked at the professor who had collapsed forward onto his desk.

"Here, now, none of that. You're missing all the fun. Your desk chair has wheels. Good. I want to roll you out here in the middle of the room. The best part is about to begin."

33

NO ONE FOUND Dr. Rider until he missed his ten o'clock class and the Dean of Faculty had to go and check. His door had two locks, the regular one and a special one Dr. Rider had installed. Only he and the dean had the key, so no janitor could get in unless the professor was there.

The dean took one look inside Dr. Rider's office, shuddered, and slammed the door shut. He used his cell phone to call 911.

Hardy got a call just after ten-thirty. He put on his uniform and charged over to the college. Upstairs he stared in amazement at Dr. Rider. He was propped up on a string base, and held in position by a dozen musical instruments of all types pushed in around him.

Doug Olson had taken the call and rushed over to the school. He notified the Chief, who was now on his way.

The victim had been strangled by thin wire that was wound around his neck and attached vertically to a ceiling fan. The wire was in segments, twitted together.

On the professor's lap lay a violin. Hardy took a closer look at it. It appeared normal except all of the strings had been cut off it.

Chief Sanderson stormed in, took one look at the scene, and called the sheriff in Hillsboro. He shook his head. "Dr. Rider. I don't believe it. No one in his right mind would do this. We have a certified psychopath on our hands."

Hardy checked the violin again. Taped to the body of the instrument was a sign he hadn't noticed before. The hand lettered sign in capital letters said "OVER-ACHIEVER."

It was the first sign of any kind that the killer had left. Hardy pointed it out to the Chief.

"What the hell does that mean? Half the people here at the college could be said to be the same."

Hardy went to check with the Dean of Faculty. Dr. Hayworth was a large man, six five, and had played basketball for the school in his college days. He explained about the double locks on Dr. Rider's door.

"The man was obsessed with security for his violin. It was the one he played for years in a symphony orchestra. He didn't want our janitors messing around in his office unless he was there."

"So there were no janitors on that floor last night?"

"Oh, yes. They still have to clean the other rooms along there. I can find out which two were on duty on that floor last night. They are probably home sleeping right now."

"I need to talk to them as soon as possible. Why was the professor here at night?"

"He had student interviews until nine o'clock. I can

check his calendar and find out who his last two students were."

"Good. That might be helpful." He gave the man his card. "Call my cell as soon as you can get the janitors and the students here so I can talk to them. It's going to take some time to get this all sorted out. The medical examiner will be here and the Sheriff's Forensic Team."

"I understand that. We will cooperate in any way that we can. I've just cancelled classes for the rest of the day."

Hardy went back to the second floor. The ME had arrived and forensics wouldn't be far behind.

"Might be some prints on that piece of paper," Officer Olson said.

"Not a chance," Hardy said. "He always wears gloves. Anyway it has to be the same guy. But the paper is interesting. Looks like there is some printing on the back side. But we can't touch it until forensic gets here."

They came five minutes later. By now Hardy knew most of them. The first thing they did was take the paper off the violin and turn it over.

"Curious," the forensic man said. "Looks like some kind of a letter." He handed it to the Chief.

Sanderson stared at it a minute, then exploded with excitement. He jumped up and down and waved the paper.

"You guys know what this is? It's a letter going out to all the members of the Barbershop Ballad Contest committee. Nobody should have this letter except members of that committee."

Hardy yelped in delight. "So, our serial killer is one of the people on the committee."

"Brilliant, Jones, your logic is wonderful. We have about fifteen members in that group. Only four of them are women, so that leaves eleven men. Well, nine men. Rudy was on the committee as well as the professor."

"Some too old and too short?" Olson asked.

"For damn sure. I'm going back to my office and check the list. You two follow up here. Check for any witnesses last night. Damn, we really have a good lead on this asshole now."

The ME had finished his work. He had untied the wire from Dr. Rider's neck and had the forensic men undo it from around the ceiling fan. He gave it to them for evaluation.

"Be damned, these are violin strings, probably the ones cut from his fiddle," the forensics man said.

The ME had given strangulation as a preliminary cause of death and the ambulance people took the body away. Students clustered in the hall and on the lawn below whispering and watching.

Hardy's cell chimed.

"Officer Jones."

"Yes, this is Dean Hayworth. We talked before. I have two students in my office ready to talk to you. I don't think they will be much help. But it's worth a try."

"I'll be right over there, Dean."

Twenty minutes later Hardy decided the dean had been right. Neither of the last two students to talk to Dr. Rider had seen anyone in the hall or on the grounds below. The last one, a girl, said she saw another student she knew on the first floor, but he was not the violent type. Hardy took the boy's name and said he'd talk to him later.

By the time Hardy's talks with the students were over, the dean brought in one of the janitors.

"His is Greg Bounty. He did the second floor of the music building last night."

Hardy shook his hand. "Mr. Bounty, did you see anyone on the second floor last night who looked suspicious?"

Bounty was about thirty, suntanned, with big brown eyes and a nervous tick around his left eye. He frowned.

"Yeah, now that you ask. I was just coming out of a room at the far end of the hall, when I see this guy come out of a room. Not sure if it was Dr. Rider's room or not but in that area. He had on a brown back pack, a black baseball cap and a tee shirt and black pants. He saw me and took off running down the other way and down the steps. Last I saw of him."

"Anything about his size?"

"Yeah, he was tall, maybe six feet and on the slender side. He sure could run"

"No look at his face?"

"Not from that distance. Then the hall isn't lighted that well."

"Thanks, Mr. Bounty. Here's my card. If you think of anything else, give me a call."

When Bounty left the dean came in. "I talked to the other janitor. He doesn't want to come over. Said he worked the first floor and didn't see anyone there after nine o'clock."

Hardy thanked him and went back to the death room. The forensic guys had finished. The college people were cleaning it up and putting the instruments away. He looked around a minute then went outside and back to the station. He wanted to see how the Chief had narrowed down the list of Barbershop people. They might have a short list of suspects.

The Chief had a grin an axe handle wide when Hardy went into his office.

"Yep, we got a list. I've eliminated all but four from the committee. Damn, they say sometimes the perp is the one you would least suspect. That's sure right this time. Here are the four guys we need to check out. I had King Broderson on the list for a while but decided he's too short."

Hardy looked at the list. He had heard of all four, but didn't know them personally. He glanced up at the Chief.

"You've checked then for any police records?"

"All pristine pure. Only two speeding tickets."

Hardy read the list: Darrel Marshal, Ivan Quinton, Lane Sinclair, and Ed Rathwood.

"What really hurts is that I've known all four of these guys for years. I've done thumbnail sketches on all four. I printed out a copy for each of the guys. Oh, where is your body guard this morning?"

"Oh, damn. When I got the call I charged right over there and didn't think to tell Fred. He'll be bummed. I'll give him a call to come in."

"Our first job now is to check out these four suspects. We do it quietly. We don't let them know that they are suspect of anything. Not quite sure how we can do that but we'll try."

"How about the old trick of taking one to lunch and getting his prints off the water glass?" Hardy asked.

"Might work. But why would we take them to lunch?"

"Your job, Chief. Something about the Barbershop Ballad thing. You can come up with some small problem or question."

"Yeah, right. I'll give Darrel a call right now. He's working on the judging. What do we do now that our chief judge is dead?"

Hardy went to his desk and saw the print out. He read it with interest.

Darrel Marshal: 38, auto salesman for Drew Chevrolet. Lived in town for at least ten years. Married, three kids. Little League coach. Avid hunter and fisherman. Good salesman. Wife works in dress shop.

Ivan Quinton: 31, medical tech in Hillsboro hospital doing X-Ray work. Assistant pastor at a Lutheran church. May become a pastor. Leads the Lutheran Teen Program in the church. Married with three kids. Stay at home mom.

Lane Sinclair: Editor of the large weekly newspaper in town. Has sold one mystery novel. Does the press releases and PR for the Ballad Contest. Married, one girl. Wife works.

Ed Rathwood, 32, owns the Rathwood Fine Furniture store. Single. Mother is rich. Good at his job. Building new store in King's shopping center. Fishing expert on coastal streams. On several community project committees. Sponsor's Boy Scout troop.

Hardy shook his head. They all looked like upstanding citizens, but one of them had to be the serial killer with absolutely no conscience. Which one of them would think that the five victims were all overachievers? He'd have to find out. He would start with Ivan. The Chief was taking Marshal. Just how did he approach him and what kind of a cock and bull story did he use to prevent suspicion?"

34

HARDY JONES LOOKED at the notes on Ivan Quinton. He was an X-Ray technician at the hospital in Hillsboro. Assistant Pastor at his Lutheran church and saving money to go to seminary to become a minister. He also led the youth group at his church.

Hardy remembered something else. For a while Ivan played baseball with a town team. Ivan was good, had been in a double A pro baseball farm team for a while before he gave it up. That was the handle. Hardy knew he could talk to him about baseball with no hint of any ulterior purpose. He'd ask the man to help them with their hitting on the little league team. Never too early to start the kids out right.

Hardy thought about it all afternoon while he was on patrol. He and his body guard went to one bike car accident that put the boy on the bike in the hospital, one dog barking complaint, and one domestic "situation" the husband called it. Hardy's shadow, Fred Newton, grinned when their shift was over.

"Best damn day I've had as a cop," Fred said. "Yep,

nothing like being an officer of the law in some little town like this. I just might hit up the chief for a full time job when this current fracas is over."

"Should be some openings," Hardy said. If we don't nail this guy soon, the city council will probably fire all of us." He told him about the four suspects and how they were going to try to question them without letting on there was a problem.

"So, you won't be with me when I talk to him. I don't want Ivan to know you're my baby sitter just in case he's the killer."

"Makes sense. But I'll be hanging out close by if anything goes wrong."

Hardy frowned. He had been worried about how to do this alone. He nodded. "Yeah, if we can work it out. This guy isn't high on my list of suspects. He's saving money to go to theological seminary to be a Lutheran pastor."

Fred laughed. "Yeah, not your usual background for a serial killer. In any case I'll be close by."

Just before he left at the end of his shift, Hardy looked up Ivan's number and called. His wife answered. Ivan was outside playing with the kids. She called him.

"Yes, Ivan Quinton here, how may I help you?"

"Ivan, Hardy Jones, we've met a few times. I've got a big favor to ask. I'm a coach of a little league team and our hitting is crazy bad. How about I buy you lunch tomorrow, and we talk."

"Mister Jones. Yes, I remember you. You're one of our policemen. You guys do a great job. I've always admired law enforcement people. As for the help on hitting, I don't know. I'm spread pretty thin as it is."

"Hey, won't take more than two hours a week. Just one practice a week and you can work wonders. None of our three coaches played baseball at all, so we know from nothing about hitting. So how about lunch tomorrow? Can we meet at the Forest Café for lunch about eleven thirty? We'll beat the crowd that way."

"I really hate to say no, Officer Jones. But the old baseball pull is getting to me. Every spring I wish that I'd given it just another year. Well, okay I'll be there. Just to talk. I'm not promising anything.'

The next morning Hardy got to the Forest Café early and talked to the waitress who would be on their table.

"Be sure we get glasses of water, and when we leave don't clear the table until I come back in after we're gone. It's important. I'll walk out with Ivan then come back in. All clear?"

Sally's eyes went wide. "Golly, Hardy. Some sort of criminal or something? I thought Ivan was going to be a minister."

"He is, so we don't want to do anything to hurt his reputation. This is just a little test. But it's important."

"Well, golly gee, Hardy. Sure. I'll make certain nobody else buses your table either."

In situations like this when Hardy was off duty and had to go somewhere, Fred followed in his car that was parked half a block down. That way Fred could be nearby in an instant. He parked near where Hardy had to go and worked inside the business or office and watched and waited.

It worked that way that noon when Hardy had left the house and Fred followed in his three year old

Pontiac. Fred came in for coffee and a donut while Hardy talked to Sally.

Then Hardy sat at the table and waited for Ivan. He was five minutes early.

Hardy realized that it didn't matter if Ivan helped with the Little League batters or not, as long as he got his fingerprints off the water glass.

It all went accruing to the plan. Ivan said he could come to three practices for about two hours one day a week and teach the boys as much as he could about the proper way to bat.

"Then it's just practice and practice and more practice. That's why pro teams always take batting practice before each game."

Ivan had a small burger and a glass of V-8 while Hardy settled for a BLT and a Coke. Sally filled their water glasses twice, and winked at Hardy. They talked baseball and about the triple-A farm team, Beavers, there in Portland. Then Ivan looked at his watch.

"I've got to run. I'll see you tomorrow afternoon about four at the Fifth Street diamond. Don't count on any miracles."

Hardy walked Ivan to his car and waved as he drove away.

Back inside Sally sat in the booth waiting for him.

"Did I do it right?" she asked.

Hardy grinned. "You were perfect. Now don't tell anyone about this okay? It is police business and you could get in trouble if you mention it."

"Mum's the word, Hardy I won't say a syllable."

Hardy took a plastic bag from his pocket, unfolded it, picked up Ivan's glass with a napkin, and lowered into the bag.

"Thanks, Sally. You did good."

Fred finished his coffee, stretched, and sauntered out the café door just ahead of Hardy. They didn't look at each other or speak. It was a hard and fast rule when Hardy was in or out of uniform.

Hardy got in his car and drove to the police station two blocks away. Chief Sanderson was there. Hardy held out the plastic sack. The Chief looked up.

"Ivan Quinton's fingerprints, Chief. I took him to lunch."

"Good. Drive them down to the lab in Hillsboro and wait and see if they find any matches." He paused. "Oh, you're off duty."

"Doesn't matter. I'll take a patrol car."

"My date with Marshal is for three o'clock. He's closing some big deal. Good luck on those prints."

"Ivan isn't a good suspect, but we've got to check them all out."

Hardy and Fred rode in the rear window tinted patrol car to the lab. Chuck was on duty and when he heard who the prints were of, he laughed.

"That would make news, a pastor as a serial killer."

"Don't get your hopes up. I just pray you can get some good prints."

He did.

There was no match with the prints they had on the killer from two of the murders.

"Not even one point match," Chuck said. "I need at least six or eight to make a case. Better luck next time."

Chuck wrote out a quick report, printed it, signed it, and gave them the printouts on the killer's prints and the prints from Ivan. Both were labeled.

"At least we cleared one," Hardy said. "Now we're down to three."

ED RATHWOOD and King Broderson took an inspection trip out to the King Shopping Center to check up on the buildings. King's was starting to look like a real store. The framing was mostly done and some walls up. The truck delivery ramp was ready in back and a contractor was working on the parking lot in front, laying out where the clumps of shrubs and tree would be and the six long rows of parking spaces. Lights would come later.

Ed was disappointed by the slow work on his store. They had run into some problems for the second floor. There would be an elevator and that was a pain. Some of the walls were going up and it was starting to take shape. Again Ed realized that he wouldn't be around to see it completed. Hell, he'd be in the south of France chasing some bikini clad beauty.

When the tour was finished, Ed and King had a cup of coffee, cried about the slowness of the project, and then went their separate ways. Ed was on his second day of watching Officer Hardy Jones. He knew he had a strange and changing schedule for work. He figured it would all take about a week to tie down when he worked and what else he did. Ed knew about the Little League coaching. No chance for anything to develop there to fit in with his planning for Jones.

He drove the little Honda he had been using lately to within half a block of the police station. He waited. Fifteen minutes later Hardy came out and took a police cruiser out of the police parking lot and headed uptown. Half a block from the station, he stopped at the curb and a man in civilian clothes got in the back seat of the cruiser. Strange.

Ed followed well back. Jones drove to the edge of town where a car had crashed through a hedge and into a tree. A single car crash. Sometime Ed wasn't looking, the civilian who got in Jones's police car evidently got out and now stayed back with a group of people who had gathered at the crash site. Strange.

He watched from a distance as Officer Jones worked the crash, getting the car pulled out of the yard, no injuries, and then taking the driver in on a drunk driving charge.

The gaggle of people around the crash faded away and Jones drove in his patrol car. Half a block away he stopped and picked up the same man he had given a ride before.

Ed chuckled. A body guard. The Chief had hired a new man and made him a ghost guard on Jones. They must think that Jones was in danger because his work on the four homicides. The newspaper story that quoted Jones about the killings might have upset the chief and made him think that Jones could be vulnerable. Why else the fit looking man who grabbed rides? He thought about the patrol car. It had tinted windows to prevent people from looking inside. And maybe to hide the body guard.

Ed followed them back to the police station then went on past and toward the store. This presented some problems for his plans for Jones but nothing he couldn't handle. If it came to that, he could do two of them at the same time. He preferred to do just Jones, to keep it pure and on the track of the overachievers. He'd see how it played out. He had to learn a lot more about the cop's movements and habits.

He drove back to the store and talked to Uriah.

"Just back from looking at the new store," Ed said. "Next time I go out there I want you to come along. See how it's going. Hey, if I fall down in front of an eighteen wheeler one of these days, you'll have to take over."

"Very good, Mr. Rathwood. However I've never known you to stumble. So it isn't a huge possibility. I'd be happy to see how the new place is coming."

Ed went up to his desk. Uriah had seemed pleased about the offer. He seldom smiled and he was one hard man to read. From what his mother said, once Ed was safely out of the country with his new name and background, she would give the store to Uriah as a thank you for all of his good work over the years. He'd been with the store in one capacity or another for Ed's dad, and now him. It must be close to thirty years. Ed shrugged. It didn't matter to him one way or the other. Ed sat at his desk, put his feet up on the corner, and smiled. Oh, yes it was going to be good to have a change of scene. His mother thought they might have some clues against him on the four homicides. He didn't think so but for ten million, he'd take his mother's advice and go to the south of France. The first thing he would do was find one of those nude beaches. He could stand some viewing time with pretty naked French girls. Oh, yes.

35

AFTER A CLOSED DOOR meeting with the City Council, Chief Sanderson was authorized to hire four new short term cops for the department.

"We have three prime suspects now and we need to track them and watch them seven twenty-four," the Chief told them. He said he couldn't reveal their names but each of the three may be implicated in some way with the crimes. He was asked how long they would be needed and the Chief told them he didn't know. Maybe a week maybe a month. It all depended how clever the killer really was. He got authorization and hired three men from the same ex-cop's firm in Hillsboro he had used before. They would work undercover and drive their own cars.

The Chief met with them in the Fifth Street park and gave them the names and addresses each was to watch.

"Don't let them know you're watching them," Chief Sanderson warned. "The whole idea is to learn what they do, where they go, and if they are watching anyone else, like the next victim."

They would make their reports by phone to the Chief. They were to call every two hours. The Chief told his four officers about the new men.

"So don't get in their way. They are not sworn law officers, but each has a gun from his guard duty work. After today maybe we'll only have two to watch. I have my postponed lunch with Darrel Marshal today."

Hardy told him about Sally at the Forest Café. "She knows the drill. Just tell her not to clear the table after you leave."

Joanie came in and talked to the Chief. He waved Hardy out of his office. They talked for about five minutes then the Chief called Hardy back in. Joanie was back at the front desk.

"Just got a curious phone call. Some man with a gruff voice just called and said he and his wife were close to blows and wanted an officer to come and settle an argument. He said he'd heard that Officer Jones was good at it and was he available."

"He asked for me by name?"

"Yes. Curious, right? Joanie said you were tied up on another call but she could send out another officer. The caller said that wouldn't do, and hung up. She didn't get a name or a number and we don't have that fancy service that tells you who is calling."

"Does sound a bit strange," Hardy said. "Who asks for a cop by name to come on a call?"

"What Joanie figured. I told her to be on the watch for anyone asking for you by name."

Hardy scratched his head. "Never happened

before. You figure this is our killer trying to get me alone somewhere?"

"Possible. Your wife called this morning saying a man called asking if you were working today. Said he was from the Little League but she didn't recognize his voice."

"Two in one day. I'm getting poplar."

"Popular and maybe on the killer's list. You be twice as careful. Ivan still with you?"

"Yes, he's attacking the donuts in the lunch room."

"Good, keep him handy. Report to me anything out of the ordinary."

"Will do. I have a date at the Halverson Grade School to talk to the fifth graders. Don't worry. Fred will be with me. I better scoot."

The talk to the kids about law and order and the usual things he always told them went well. The kids had dozens of questions and everyone wanted to see his gun. He unloaded it and showed it to them. Fred had stayed in the patrol car with the tinted windows and watched the parking lot.

When Hardy came out after the talk, Fred shrugged.

"Not a sign of any other cars arriving or leaving, and no foot traffic. I'd say we're safe here."

"Good. I get any calls?"

"Joanie called and said get in touch with her when you're done here."

Hardy called her on the radio.

"Hardy we have two car crashes. Bob is on the first one. The other one is at Second Street East and Fifth Avenue. That's yours. Only about ten minutes old. Any trouble?"

"Smooth as an ice cream sundae. I'm moving."

The crash turned out to be a sideswipe with the second rig taking off before the first car's driver could get a license plate.

"It was an older Toyota pickup, maybe ten years old. Blue, and with the box loaded with firewood. All I can tell you."

Hardy helped the man write out an accident report and said he'd file it at the office. The man's Chevy was bashed in along the driver's side, but the man wasn't hurt.

"Sure wish I had that girl's license plate."

"A woman was driving?"

"Oh, yea. Thought I told you. She looked to be about sixteen, but may be older. She didn't even slow down."

Fred had stayed in the patrol car's back seat with the door cracked open three inches for a fast move if needed.

The rest of the day went by without any problems. Then Hardy realized it was four o'clock.

"Damn, it's Little League practice day," Hardy said. "Our batting coach is going to be there." Hardy called Joanie telling her he was on public service call for the rest of his shift.

Joanie laughed. "Good, Hardy. Get those baseball kids in line. See you tomorrow."

On the way to the Little League field, Fred yelped. "I think we have a follower. A new black Lexus has been with us for three blocks. Just hangs back there but turns whenever we do. Yep, he made that last turn with us."

Hardy slowed, turned to the curb, and stopped along a residential street.

Fred grinned. "Good play, stopping. Now we see what he does."

The Lexus slowed as well and a hundred feet behind them turned into a house driveway.

"Five will get you ten he doesn't live there," Fred said. "We have any binoculars?"

"Got a pair, but left them in my car. A pair of Bushnell twelve fifties that will knock your socks off."

"Damn. I should have had his license. He's still in the car can we wait him out?"

"I'll give him five minutes."

Two minutes later the Lexus backed out of the driveway and turned the other way, going away from the police car.

"Make a note of that for your report," Hardy said. "That jerk was following us for sure. New black Lexus, no plate."

The practice was underway when they arrived. Ron Warner stood to one side watching. Hardy talked to the other coach who was there and a minute later he had all the boys in a bunch telling them about Ivan Quinton's professional baseball career and how he was going to help them with batting.

Ivan took over and began explaining some basics. He was good with the kids. Hardy relaxed and tried to remember what Ivan was teaching.

ED PULLED his Lexus in his private parking space behind the store and nodded. He turned off the radio police scanner he had bought the day before. His test run had been good. He caught the assignment of Officer Jones to the crash site and had arrived before he did. Yes, the scanner could very well fit into his plans for Mr. Jones.

Upstairs in his office, Ed tried to work out a time, place, and method for his surprise party for Officer Hardy Jones. Nothing seemed to be fitting together. He had to figure some way to get Hardy alone, without his body guard. Then he had to find a time and a place to make it happen. It would have to be on a work night for Jones. Then watch the scanner for the first call that might work out. Nothing downtown nothing on a highly traveled street. He could call in an accident at the right place. That would be risky, but it might get the job done. Jones wore a gun, a Glock automatic with fourteen rounds in the magazine. Maybe it would be fitting if Jones went down with a gun shot. Not terribly inventive but fitting. He'd work on that.

Maybe at the new building out at the King Shopping Center. They were past the point where they needed a night watchman. So there was no guard on site now after the troops left. No night crews to rush the job done. Yes, that just might be the spot. He could call in saying that a truck at the site with four men stealing things out of the King Grocery. This one was going to take some work but it would be worth it. Yeah, a week or so and he would be off to France and those delicious naked French beauties on the beach.

He heard Uriah coming up the stairs. He always made noise coming up so he didn't take his boss by surprise. He came in with his usual deference.

"Mr. Rathwood you had two phone calls. One from your mother asking if she should plan on having you to dinner tonight. She needed a reply by five o'clock. The other call was from Beaverton. The man said he had an extremely exiting special sale on for tonight. He hoped that you could stop by and evaluate the merchandise. He said seven thirty would be fine. If you can make it, you should call him back at the usual number."

Ed smiled. "Uriah, I don't tell you often enough how much I rely on you and lean on you for so many things around the store. I really am grateful. Call mother and tell her I have a meeting tonight with some suppliers about the new store."

"Yes, Mr. Rathwood. I'll do that right away. Is there anything else I can do for you? A soft drink, a cold bottle of water?"

"No, but thank you. I'm fine." Uriah turned and went back down the stairs. Ed reached for the phone.

TWO HOURS LATER, Ed finished a big steak dinner at the best restaurant in Beaverton called El Greco and then drove three miles out to the north of Beaverton to a quiet suburb street. He parked four housed down, as usual, and walked quickly to the rear door of a four bedroom ranch style house. The door was not locked. Ed walked in, went to the living room, and was greeted by a portly man with sweat beading his forehead.

"Ah, you made it. This is something exciting and unusual. I know you like the oriental type and not too used. This one is not really broken in yet, she's thirteen, and may give you a fight. But then I know you like that too." He gave Ed a key.

"It's room three. Oh, she's Le Ling."

Ed walked down the short hall and unlocked the

door with the big three on it. He pushed the panel open slowly with his foot against the bottom of it. The door was open only a foot when something slammed into it from inside. His boot and shoulder took the blow and then he pushed back hard. He heard a cry from the other side and stepped into the room.

A small Chinese girl lay on the carpeted floor where she had fallen. She looked up at him with rage and fury spilling from her face.

"Ah, so. You must be Le Ling. It's good to meet you."

36

BY THE TIME Hardy came to work the next morning the station was buzzing. The Chief had called in all four of his regulars and Fred sat in.

"Well, we're down to two suspects, if that damn Barbershop Contest letter was for real and if it went to the killer. My contact with Darrel Marshal cleared him. His prints off the glass turned out to be no possible match to the killer's. So we now have Ed Rathwood and Lane Sinclair.

"On the surface it would look like Ed is the best bet. He's single and sleeps around. But he's also a pillar of the community, has that big store, building a bigger one, and then there are the millions that he'll inherit from his mother. So where is his motivation?

"Sinclair on the other hand is a working stiff, editor of the local weekly newspaper, married with two kids, and a working wife.

"Jones, you might have a connection here. You could go down and tell him to be sure not to use your name in connection with the serial murder case. Tell him about cops who have been blown away when they shoot off their mouths too much about a killer or a case. Some of these psychopaths are sensitive. You can always do the lunch thing again with the glass for his prints."

"I'll go down about eleven, have a talk and if nothing shows up to clear him, I'll do lunch," Hardy said.

Fred spoke up. "Chief, I don't think this shadow operation is working for us. If this killer is as good as he seems to be, he must know that I'm on hand with Hardy every minute. Why don't we just forget the stealth and let me go side by side with Hardy wherever he goes. No secret I'm there with him so take your best shot."

The Chief thought about it a moment then looked at Hardy.

"Yeah, Chief. I think he isn't fooled by our subterfuge. He must know Fred is my cover. Let's bring him out and put him in uniform."

"Okay, done. The rest of you pay close attention to what's going on. Any little thing might tip the scales one way or the other."

A half hour later Hardy and Fred went on a call about a cat up a tree. When they got there they found out the cat was a year old female cougar that was hungry and frightened. Hardy called Joanie who called County Animal Control. They had a truck in the area and would be a the address in half an hour.

"So we keep the cat from killing anyone and from any gung ho hunter from shooting the cat," Hardy said.

Ten minutes later a man in a red vest showed up with a 30.06 rifle and a pocket full of cartridges.

"I can put her down and dead with two shots," the man said.

Hardy shook his head. "Not a chance. Animal Control is coming. They will either tranquilize the cat or catch her in a net. I'm going to ask you to unload the rifle."

"Damn. My first chance to get a cougar and some cop stops me. Just ain't fair."

"You have a hunting license, sir?"

"Hell, not hunting, just walking round. See you later."

Fred chuckled. "Never had that problem in Portland. This is one strange little town."

"We like it that way."

The county men came and tranquilized the animal with one dart shot from a special gun and then three of the men caught the hundred pound cougar as she fell ten feet out of the tree. They put her in a cage in one of the trucks and took off.

"Where to for the kitty?" Fred asked.

"Take her out into the mountains, over by Wilson River, probably and let her go. Hey, time we went down to the newspaper and talked to Lane Sinclair. He's the one of the four I know the best. Went to school with him."

Lane Sinclair was a slight man with prematurely gray hair he kept cut short. He had just finished the lead story of the week on the Barbershop Ballad Contest. He looked up from his desk and grinned.

"But officer, I didn't know I was going that fast."

"Doesn't matter Sinclair, you're going up the river for five to ten." Hardy laughed. "How's it going, Lane?"

"I'm doing good. What I want to know is how is the investigation coming along with our serial killer?"

"Need to talk to you about that, Lane," Hardy said. "Oh, this is Officer Fred Newton, new man."

"Good to meet you. Sit."

"About the story. I did an interview couple of weeks ago and it was on the front page. My Chief was upset. Said I was setting myself up to be the next victim of the killer. These guys don't like to get talked about in print."

"Just doing our job, Hardy. You know that."

"Right, but I'm asking as a personal favor not to use my name in any story about the murders. The Chief will appreciate it and so will I. I'm not good copy anyway."

"I don't remember quoting you since that first story. So I see no reason we should use your name now. Maybe after you nail this sonofabitch."

"Sounds good to me, Lane. Hey, where did you get the good tan all of a sudden?"

"About time you noticed. I took the family to San Diego for a week. Sun all over the place. Went out of our minds. What a beautiful area. Just got back two days ago. Spent a fortune, but it's just money." He pulled out a folder and spread out a batch of color pictures. "Want to see my pictures?"

"Maybe later. You stayed a whole week?"

"Yeah, after you fly that far you need to stay a week."

"So you missed out on the fourth kill of our serial guy. The music man himself at the college, Dr. Rider."

"Yes, herd about it on the TV, and what a shock.

We got back two days after he was murdered. We remade the whole front page for the paper that week."

"I remember it. A good job. When is your next novel coming out? I understand you're doing mysteries now."

"Writing them and getting them published are two different worlds. I have three looking for publishers. Might never see print. Way it goes."

"Good luck with them. Well, we better get back to work. And thanks for keeping my name out of the paper. Glad you enjoyed San Diego. Take care now."

They were back in the patrol car before Hardy let out a yelp of joy. "Wow. I'm glad it isn't Lane. H's really a good one. Now we have just one suspect to watch."

"That would be Ed the furniture store guy?"

"Right, good old Ed Rathwood."

When Hardy told the Chief about Lane Sinclair's air tight alibi, he gave a sigh of relief.

"I hoped it wasn't Lane. Known him a long time. So now we have just one, Ed Rathwood. The thing we don't have is any solid evidence. The fingerprint will be good once we take them but I'm not sure they would be enough for our picky District Attorney to bring charges. What would be solid and winning evidence would be to catch him in the act."

"Good, Chief, and you can be the victim," Hardy said.

"Wouldn't work. He picks the victims. Good of you to volunteer me." There was a pause. Chief Sanderson looked around at his four men. He had already sent two of his temporary watcher cops over to city hall to pick up their checks. He'd go with seven men.

"Time to get down to some strategy. How well do

any of you know Ed Rathwood?" He looked around. Most of the men shook their heads.

"I bought a couch there a year ago. But I dealt with his man Uriah," Douglas Olson said.

"What about Uriah? Any of you know him?"

Hardy looked up. "He goes to my church, so I've a nodding acquaintance with him, but that's about all. We say hello, how are you, and move on." Nobody else knew him at all.

"So we're back to Ed," Chief Sanderson said. "Last time I saw him he wore latex gloves like medical people do. He said a friend of his picked up hepatitis just by shaking hands. He wasn't about to do the same thing."

"So there goes our chance to get fingerprints from a lunch," Long said.

"Wonder if he thinks we have fingerprints from some of the kills and he doesn't want to risk getting printed," Hardy said."

"A good chance," the Chief said. "We've said this killer is smart. I'd put Ed right up there for being both smart and careful."

"So what do we do next?" Long asked.

"Scare him," Fred said. "Make him think we know more than we do. Maybe he'll do something stupid, or even run."

"How about a shot at his DNA?" Young asked. "We're back to lunch. Let him eat with his gloves on. He has to drink something. Coffee, water, a Coke. His DNA is going to be on the rim of that cup or glass."

"Yes," Chief Sanderson said with delight. "I'll try to set up a lunch with him today about the judges. They are having some trouble getting that mess all cleared up since Dr. Rider died. Get out of here and let me make some phone calls."

The troops scattered. Hardy and Bob Long were on the duty for today. They checked with Joanie but there were no calls to go on. They worked on written reports and then tried to get some good ideas how they could scare Ed into making a mistake.

By noon they both had run out of ideas that wouldn't work.

They had three calls then and were busy with small town police work for the rest of their shift.

The two temp watchers had been reassigned to keep tabs on Ed Rathwood. Chief Sanderson briefed them on his store and one or two of his cars. Will Blakely had been a homicide sergeant in Portland for ten years before he retired. Now he took the day shift on Ed. They would work twelve hour tours.

Will drove a year old Mazda. He parked across the street and walked past Ed's store. He'd been given a description of Ed and spotted him talking to an older man near the front of the place. Will kept going, then returned to his car and settled in for a long wait.

He was still there when Ed came out the front door at ten minutes to twelve and walked a half block to the Forest Café. A few minutes later he saw Chief Sanderson arrive. This was the lunch with the suspect the Chief had talked about. Good.

ED HAD BEEN WORKING with the rest of the judging committee and brought Chief Sanderson up to date.

"Yeah, we hired two men to come help us. They

will judge but wouldn't do it for free. So we have our total number of judges. Now if the system that the committee and Dr. Rider worked out functions, we'll be home free."

"That's good. I've been worried about it. Is coffee and a Danish all the lunch you ordered?"

"Right, I don't want to get fat. I'm only ten pounds over my playing weight. I want to keep it that way."

Fifteen minutes later they finished lunch and the Chief grabbed the check. He watched in surprise as Ed wiped off the knife and fork he had used with a paper napkin. Then he wiped half a dozen times around the rim of the coffee cup.

"That surprises you, doesn't it?" Ed asked. "One of my best friends got hepatitis at a restaurant. That's why I wear these medial gloves. Then I wipe off my germs from the fork and the cup so I don't infect anyone else with any illness I may have. My way of keeping the people safe."

Ed left a five dollar tip and they walked outside together.

"Good getting that judging thing off my mind," Chief Sanderson said. The chief walked to his car and Ed hiked back toward his store. The Chief watched Ed go. Ed sounded sincere about wiping off his germs. But was he? Did he know that the police might have DNA from one of the killings and his own would match? The Chief figured Ed was smart enough to be sure not to spread his DNA around. There went another easy way to tie down a killer, maybe enough hard evidence to get a search warrant, and an arrest warrant from the DA. The Chief was stumped. Just what the hell should he do now?

37

WHEN HARDY GOT HOME that evening about six, Cindy was upset. Her face was a little pale and her eyes had a worried look that Hardy had seen before. She couldn't keep her hands still and when she kissed him, she put her arms around him and didn't want to let loose.

"Honey, what's the matter?"

"Somebody is watching the house. I saw him out the front window when I was cleaning the living room this morning. Then about noon he was there again, walking past on the other side of the street. It had to be the same man, but he had on different clothes. I went out, puttered around in the flower bed, and he left and didn't come back."

She let him go and wiped silent tears from her cheeks. "Are we in any danger, Hardy? Is that why Fred is staying so close?"

He told her the whole thing about the Chief's concern.

"So, Fred is just a little insurance, that's all. Not

even this guy would be so dumb to try anything against a cop."

"You better be right. I plan on having you around for another fifty years." She closed her eyes and lifted her brows. "I've been so shaken that I didn't even get us dinner."

"No problem, pretty lady. We'll go out, to a real restaurant, not to Bob Biggest Burgers."

THAT NOON ED walked away from the café with a big grin. He had seen through the Chief's question about the contest judging. That didn't take a rocket scientist. His latex gloves must have given the cop a turn. Then when he wiped off the "germs" and the DNA from his fork and the coffee cup, he had seen the briefest little reaction from the Chief.

He walked back to the store. He had some book work and ordering that he had to get done. It would take most of the afternoon. As soon as he had that taken care of, he would have a good dinner, and then do some research. He wanted to scout out the new store in the King Shopping Center after the workers had left. He needed to find just the right spot in the new store to take care of Hardy Jones.

About seven o'clock that night he went to the King Shopping Center. It was still light enough to see. The floor was down on about half of the second story. That was good. He might use that for his staging area. This one was going to be by the gun, but it had to have some class, some polish, something different than a straight assassination.

What would be the perfect ploy to get the cop out

here? Stealing or maybe a teen age drinking party? That sounded better. Jones had a reputation among students for breaking up beer busts. That might get him rolling. Yes, it could be on the second floor with candles for light and lots of beer. Only when he got there, Hardy Jones would not find anyone but Ed waiting for him.

What weapon? It would have to be special, maybe unique. He thought of the old time Western .45 caliber Colts he had in his collection. He could sacrifice one. He wished he had a pirate blunderbuss, but he hadn't found one that he liked. Certainly it wouldn't be the officer's issue weapon.

Ed came down from the second floor and saw a pickup parked in front of the unfinished King's Center Grocery. It looked like two men were loading something in it. He had driven one of his Jeeps today, the one with a strong front bumper and a winch. He drove up slowly toward the pickup. The two men saw him coming and tried to get in the rig quickly. They weren't fast enough.

Ed rammed his front bumper against the pickup's front tire and fender, smashing it in and stopping the rig where it had been backing up. The fender had slammed into the front tire and smashed it inward. The pickup could not be driven.

The two men screamed at him then took off running. Ed laughed. He got out of his Jeep and inspected his front bumper. A six inch scratch showed on the chrome. He backed away and drove out of the construction site the long way, then into town. He'd let the workers find the foiled theft and the smashed up pickup the next morning.

Ed drove home. He would look over his collection

of firearms in the second bedroom in his wing. He had over a hundred firearms of all types and styles. Even a few that were illegal. No matter, no one had ever seen them but him. He would select the weapon to introduce to Forest Glen Police Officer Hardy Jones. He was smiling as he went into the house though the front door. His mother must have heard him drive in. She waited for him.

"Nice of you to come home now and then, Edward. How is your project coming along?"

"Progressing. As you said, I have to be ultimately careful with this one. No time to make any mistakes this late in the game."

His mother's face flared in anger. "Oh, Edward. What am I going to do with you? All of this is just a game to you, isn't it? But a serious deadly game that you must win. How soon can you get away for New York and Paris?"

"I told you, it will take some more time. I even had lunch on Chief Sanderson today. I think he was fishing. But I wore my latex gloves and wiped my DNA off the coffee cup. Not to worry, Mommy Dearest."

"Thought I should tell you, Edward. The police have found fingerprints at two of the murder sites. They arc yours, of course. Now they will try to match them with any suspects that they have. You must be one if the Chief took you to lunch."

"Just how do you know this?"

"Talkative old woman. The Chief's wife just can't help but run off at the mouth. She tries to impress the rest of us at the bridge table. So she talks and talks. A lot about the case and what she hears about it from her husband."

"They won't get my prints. None are on file with the county, state, or the FBI. They can look in all the files they want to. I won't let them get near anything that I have touched without the gloves. Tomorrow I wipe down all my cars, and my tools, and everything at the office. I don't want them coming at me with a search warrant."

Elmira Rathwood gave a little sigh and her face showed more emotion than Ed had seen there in years.

"Dear Edward. You may not believe this, but I still love you. Knowing who you are and all the terrible things you have done, I still love you. A mother's curse I guess."

Ed stood there in the living room stunned by his mother's confession. He had never even suspected that her feelings ran this deep. He had always thought of her as a taker, not a giver, one who took what she wanted, when she wanted it, and to hell with everyone else. Even him.

"Now, let's not get maudlin about this, Mother. We have our arrangements and I'll get that airline ticket to New York just as soon as possible, maybe in three or four days. I promise you that. Then you'll be free and well rid of me."

"It's not only that. I worry about you getting caught. Think what it would do to me, the fall out, the social outcast sort of thing." She brightened. "You say three or four days. That's good. Let me get your other life papers, cards, background, bank books, and the whole thing. I have it all packed in a thin leather case so you can study the names and dates and places. You must memorize your background so you'll be convincing living as another person"

"Yes, now would be a good time. You know I'm a fast study. I'll have it all memorized before I leave. Oh, speaking of leaving. I'll need a few thousand in cash when I go. I'd say ten thousand in hundreds will do nicely until I get established and my new credit cards and money transferred into my new bank accounts. Damn, wish that I'd paid more attention to my French language classes at college."

"You'll do well. You do pick up things quickly. Let me go get that material for you. I think I have five thousand in the wall safe. I can give you that now and get the rest tomorrow."

"Great. Now about the store. You inherited it from Dad when he passed. So you can sell it to Uriah for one dollar, right?"

"That's what I was planning on doing"

"Good. Could you write out a statement to that effect? Then if anything goes wrong, you can still get the store to Uriah."

His mother frowned. "What could go wrong? I'll be here even if you're in France."

"Nothing will go wrong, but I'd rest a little easier if I knew that Uriah was going to get the store. All you have to do is write it out on your stationery, date it, sign it, and put it with your papers. Easy. Hey, I'm getting out of your life. This seems like a little thing I'm asking you to do."

Elmira sighed. "I don't see why..." She stopped.

"All right. We can do it right now if that will keep you from yapping about it." She laughed. "Yes, let's do it right now."

Five minutes later it was done. She put it in an envelope, sealed it, and put it in her wall safe. Then she took out bank wrapped one hundred dollar bills. There were two wrappings with fifty bills in each one.

"There you are, a hundred one hundred dollar bills. That'd be ten thousand. It's my emergency money so I'll have to replace it."

"And the ten million?"

"That's all taken care of. Each of your new bank accounts has been wired two million. I'll send you the rest when you need it."

"You said ten…"

"Hush, you will get it as you need it. Now let's not talk about money any more. It gives me a headache."

Ed checked his fury. She had said ten million. He struggled to keep his voice calm. "Yes, Mother. Now I need to go work on my gun collection. I won't be taking it with me. After a reasonable amount of time, you can advertise it and sell all the weapons to some dealer. One revolver needs some repair work on it. I'll see you for breakfast, Mother. Tomorrow is going to be a big day for me.

She looked up. "You're going to do it tomorrow?"

"No, not tomorrow, but I'll be making some big decisions tomorrow about the how and when. Good night mother. Pleasant dreams."

38

THE NEXT MORNING, Ed was nervous and fidgety. He couldn't settle down to anything at work. He was anxious to get Hardy done once and for all.

All of his planning about how to kill the cop now seemed wrong, too slow, too far away. He had to do it quicker. Why not today? Yes, he could do it today. He was ready. Just a little planning and then go, go, go. Why not a real shootout near the edge of town? He went to his Jeep and checked the police scanner he had set on the Forest Glen radio frequency.

Yes, Hardy and Olson were on duty today. He drove home, took out his 30.06 with the ten power scope on top and one of his Colt revolvers. He loaded the Colt with.45 rounds, and took a dozen rounds for the rifle. Then he drove around looking for a good spot for a shootout. He found it near the north part of town, out toward Banks. A new subdivision with only two houses finished, but nobody working on it today. It was called Forest View Homes.

Ed checked the scanner again. He waited until

Olson was sent out on a call. It was just past ten in the morning. He parked behind an almost finished house and made his call. He changed his voice making it sound soft and unsure.

"Hello, police? I don't know if I should call or not but it looks like some men are stealing lumber from a construction site."

"Thanks for calling. Where is the site?"

"Oh, it's the new Forest View Homes out north of town on Henry Street."

"Yes, I know the area. We'll send an officer out there right away. Thank you for the call. Could I have your name and phone number?"

"What? What? I'm losing your signal. Sorry. Goodbye."

He turned up the volume on the scanner and waited.

Two minutes later the radio sounded.

"Joanie, I'm done with that fender bender on Pacific Highway. Anything else?"

Joanie told him about the theft in progress.

"Right, I'm on it. Out."

Ed tried to figure from which end of the two block long street the cop would come from. He decided it would be from the east. He moved his Jeep so the house would hide it, then took the Colt and the rifle with him and found a good sniper spot behind a three foot high stack of concrete blocks. It gave him a good field of fire to the east. He'd stop the cop car well out of pistol range so he'd have a total advantage. It was a seven minute wait before he saw the police car pull into the just paved street in the subdivision. It was a block and a half away. It moved slowly evidently Hardy was checking each area to look for the looters.

When it got to fifty yards, he'd put a round through the windshield. Hell, one round might do it. The police car came forward. Ed sighted in on it through the scope. When it was five houses down, he fired. He brought the scope back on the target to check. The round had smashed through the windshield shattering it. He couldn't see anyone in the front seat. He pulled the rifle back out of sight and waited.

In the patrol car, Hardy saw and heard the windshield crack into a thousand lines as the safety glass held the two panes of glass together. A gaping four inch hole showed near the center. He dove to the passenger's side of the car and reached back and turned off the engine. He waited. There was no second shot. A rifle somewhere ahead.

"We been shot at," Fred said from the back seat where he had been taking a nap. "You hit, Hardy?"

"No, not a scratch. How the hell can we fight against a rifleman with our pistols?"

"We stay low and see what he does. He might think he nailed you with that first round. Even so he'd have to come and make sure." Fred edged up to look out the side window.

"We have some blocks and bricks and a stack of lumber over on my side of the street. I might be able to get behind him. I can open the door and make a dash for those blocks. Only about twenty feet away. Good chance he couldn't get off a shot. Looks like our best bet."

"No, Fred. I can't let you do that." Before Hardy

finished his protest, he heard the car's right hand rear door jolted open.

Fred didn't think about it twice. He slammed open the car's door and hit the ground running, charging for the blocks. He heard the rifle speak again but the round missed him six feet behind. He dove in back of the blocks and caught his breath. When he left the car he automatically drew his Glock pistol. He edged to the side of the blocks and looked around. There were five more stacks of blocks ahead of him screening out the view of the first house that looked nearly finished. He surged around the side of the blocks and ran to the next stack waiting to be used on for the next house. It was about fifty feet away. He skidded to a stop behind the blocks. There had been no shot. The gunman had no way of seeing him or knowing what he was doing. Good. He made it to the next three stacks of blocks the same way.

This time when he looked around the blocks he saw that he was about fifty feet from the nearly finished house. It too, had a stack of blocks in front. He looked closer and could see a pair of legs extending from the far side of the blocks.

Fred estimated the distance. He had never been an expert shot with a pistol. How far? Maybe forty feet. Fifteen yards. They had a twenty yard target at the gun range where he went. He'd hold the weapon with both hands and fire as fast as he could. He should be able to get off five or six shots before the man could react. Worth a try.

He moved as far forward as he could next to the blocks and sighted in. He raised the sighs a little for the distance then held his breath and fired. He got off five shots before the legs vanished around the blocks. Fred didn't know if he hit the man. At least he scared him.

Fred heard four more shots from the rifle in quick order. The bushwhacker must be firing at the patrol car. He hoped that Hardy had gone to the floor in the front seat so he'd have part of the engine to protect him.

Fred pulled his cell phone from his pocket and punched up Hardy's number on the speed dial. The law officer came on at once.

"Fred, is that you?"

"Right, how are you? Those last shots hit you?"

"I'm kissing the floorboards here. Did you hit him?"

"Don't know. Only target I had were his legs."

"Hey, there he goes. He's leaving the blocks and running for that finished house."

"I'll try to get closer. Maybe I can get another shot at him."

"Don't do anything foolish, Fred."

"Not me. I'm moving."

Fred came to his feet, looked at the last stack of blocks ahead, and then sprinted for them. No shots came. He looked around them at the finished house.

"He's running around the house," Hardy said on the phone. "He's got the rifle and ran around the corner of the finished house. Tall guy, slender, could be Ed."

Fred looked around the blocks again and saw a figure vanish past the far side of the house. It was a two story affair with a porch in front.

Then he heard a motor start

"Hear an engine start. He must have a car back there," Fred said into his cell. "I'm moving."

Fred got to the far corner of the house in time to see a Jeep blasting out of the yard onto the new street and heading west. It was fifty feet away but Fred emptied his Glock magazine at the retreating vehicle.

Fred's cell chimed. It was Hardy.

"Those last shots from him killed the engine. Won't start. I'll use the radio and call for a backup and a tow truck. Could you ID the culprit?"

"No chance. He was too far away. But he could have been Ed Rathwood. Same body type about the same height."

ED RATHWOOD SWORE at himself as he charged down the new blacktop to the connecting street, then slowed for his short drive back to town. His left leg hurt like fire. First the dam thigh wound, now he had a bullet in his calf. It was bleeding. He couldn't stop to wrap it up. He couldn't go to the hospital. He couldn't go to any of the doctors in town. He'd just have to take care of it himself. He went home and called to his mother.

She came into the kitchen carrying a book.

"Edward. From the looks of your face, it didn't go well."

"Not well at all, Mother. How are you at digging bullets out of raw flesh?"

39

ED'S MOTHER looked at him sternly. "I thought I told you to be careful. You could really be messing up all of my plans. Did they get your license plate number?"

"I have some used license plates I borrowed from a junked car, so it wouldn't help them. Now my damn leg. It's bleeding all over the kitchen."

"I can see that, Edward. Don't bother me with the obvious. And no I am not good at digging bullets out of raw flesh. Actually the sight of human blood scares the hell out of me. However, I have a friend here in town who used to be a nurse. Spent some army time in Viet Nam. She owes me several favors. Now is a good time to collect. Wrap a towel around that leg to stop the bleeding and we'll take a ride. No, she won't say a word about a bullet wound to the police. Let's get started."

BOB YOUNG LED a tow truck into the construction site a half hour after the shooting. The tow truck driver was in his twenties, and curious about the reason the car wouldn't start. He looked under the hood and shook his head.

"Heard it was a rifle that did the damage.

Just don't know what it was. You want a tow to the Ford dealer in town?"

Hardy said he did and watched the kid hook up the tow. Then he and Fred rode with Young heading for headquarters.

"Don't know if it will do any good but I found four spent 30.06 cartridges back there by that stack of concrete blocks," Fred said. "If we ever have a rifle like that, we could check it to match the ejector marks on the brass."

"Good thinking, buddy," Hardy said. "Guess I was so shook up I didn't even think about finding the brass. Hey, I've never been shot at before."

When they pulled in at the station they were just ahead of Sally from the Forest Café.

"Hi, guys. Is the Chief in?"

"His car is here, so he should be. Hope it's important. He gets grouchy sometimes this time of day."

"Oh, I think he'll be pleased."

"Right this way, Sally. I'll escort you personally to the great chief's teepee."

Sally laughed. "I didn't realize you were an Indian, Hardy."

The Chief looked up when they came in. He stood and said hi to Sally.

"I have something for you, Chief. I remember how you tried to get fingerprints from people at the café. Then I saw Ed Rathwood wearing those latex gloves.

Now that was strange. Then I remembered about the prints. I watch lots of TV shows about police."

"So?" the Chief asked.

"So he came in yesterday bowing and scraping and I saw it was some big shot business man from back east by the way he was dressed. Ed was giving him a pitch about how well he could handle the man's line of furniture sold nationally. Ed did not have on the plastic gloves, nor did he wipe off his cup. As soon as they left I picked up his water glass with a napkin and put it in a plastic sack. Did the same thing with his coffee cup." She held out a plastic grocery bag. "We got so busy after that that I forgot them. A day won't hurt will it? So here they are."

The Chief jumped up and let out a bellow of delight. "Darling Sally. If these are his prints, we owe you a huge debt. In fact I'll never eat anywhere but at the Forest Cafe and insist that you serve me. Then I can tip you outrageously."

"I think he's pleased," Sally said. "Hey, hope it helps. My break time is over. Got to get back to the old salt mine."

The Chief gave her a hug then kissed her cheek and she blushed. She waved and hurried out of his office. The Chief turned to Bob Long. "Get these down to Hillsboro and tell them you'll wait for the prints. See if they match our killer's prints. Have them put the cup out for a DNA test. And move it man, we may just have nailed down our killer."

After Bob left, Hardy told the Chief about his shootout. "That's about it. If he was Ed he could have a slug in one of his legs."

. . .

IN HILLSBORO at the County Sheriff's crime lab, they sent the cup out by UPS to the state for a DNA test. At the same time another man was lifting the prints off the glass and printing them out, then checking them against the prints in the evidence file of the killer's prints.

"We have an exact match," Lonny said. "I'd say we have eight or nine points to match. That's almost perfect. Good evidence in a trial."

Long called the Chief. "It's a perfect match. Ed is our killer."

"Great, I'm calling the DA now and asking him for an indictment, and asking our County judge there for a search warrant. You stand by and go to the judge's office if he gives us a yes. We could be inside the Rathwood Manor house before supper."

Hardy signed on for another shift so he could be in on the search warrant serving. But the judge they needed was out of town today. He'd be back tomorrow and his secretary would tell him about the request.

Hardy listened to the Chief talking to the DA in Hillsboro. The gist of it was that the DA wanted more hard evidence than the fingerprints. He said wait until after the search warrant and see what they discovered in his house.

The Chief put the phone down softly then slapped his hand down hard on his desk top.

"Damnit. With a warrant we could pick him up before he knew what was happening – about three A.M. tomorrow morning. Now we wait."

It was a slow afternoon and evening for Forest Glen Police. One car crash, a house fire that was put out before Hardy and his fire truck arrived. Then nothing.

He and Fred cruised around letting the public know they were on guard.

Olson had taken another car crush just as it got dark. When Hardy got back from the fire, he went on patrol again. The radio came on and the night girl called Hardy.

"Up to you on a domestic disturbance call. It's at 145 West Third Avenue. Husband called and he said his wife locked herself in the bathroom and she won't come out. She says she wants some police protection and then she's going to a shelter for battered women."

Hardy headed for Third Avenue. Fred looked at Hardy in the faint light of the patrol car. It was dark outside.

"I don't know about this call. It's what I used to call questionable. It sounds too complete. If my wife locked herself in the bathroom, and screamed at me, I'd be half out of my gourd and not coherent. This guy had all the answers."

"You think it's Ed setting me up again? But how would he know that I'd be given the call?"

"Easy. I've had more than one guy who used a police scanner to monitor police calls. All it would take would be a little radio tuned to the police frequency. He'd know that Olson was on one call. So he'd wait a minute then make his call because he knows you're on duty tonight."

"How would he know that?"

"Hardy if you're a target, he knows everything about you. Believe me."

"So we make the call?"

"Cautiously. No siren, no red lights. We park five or six houses away and walk up. Then we slip up on the house from the side. At the door, we crouch down on both sides of it, then ring the bell."

Hardy looked at him a second then nodded. "Okay, Fred. You've been a cop a lot longer than I have. We do it your way."

"And we both have our Glocks out and ready to fire."

They did it that way, both against the front of the house next to the door. Hardy rang the bell. No response. He rang it twice more.

Then gunfire erupted inside the house and a dozen slugs jolted through the glassed in section of the door waist to head high.

"Submachine gun," Fred bellowed. He put three rounds through the broken out glass window in the door. "I'll get the back." He jumped away from the door and ran to the side yard and to the back. There was no side fence. Just as he got there he saw a figure climbing over an eight foot wooden fence at the back of the lot. He sent one shot at the figure but missed. Hardy came running around. They both looked at the fence.

"No way can I go over that," Fred said. "Maybe twenty years ago. Not today."

"He has too much of a head start now. Probably has a car in front of that house back there."

Back at the front of the house they tried the door knob. The door was unlocked. Inside there were no lights on. Hardy flipped a switch and lights glowed. There was no furniture. They saw two For Sale signs in the front room. They found brass on the floor in front of the door.

"Sounded like an Uzi," Fred said. "Those things can get deadly."

Back at the station, Hardy wrote out a report on the assault, printed out two copies, and filed one in his own notebook. They stayed on until midnight then checked out.

At Hardy's house he pulled into the garage past the automatic door then closed it. Fred said he'd watch outside for a while. He hunkered down in some shrubs near the front of the house so he could see up and down both sides of the street.

As he waited, two families came home. One motorcycle purred in quietly and rolled into a garage. Three more cars drove by.

An hour later, Fred gave up and went into the Jones house through the side door into the garage. He wondered why Ed was changing his methods. Usually he planned carefully. Now he seemed like he was playing it by ear, taking chances, and in a rush to kill Hardy. A sobering idea drilled through his brain. The guy was a psychopath, who wouldn't mind killing two if he needed to, just so he got Hardy. Fred beat down the thought. He'd been in dangerous situations before. Fred went to sleep on the couch about two a.m., sure that the rest of the night would be quiet.

40

THE CHIEF DROVE to Hillsboro's County
Courthouse the next morning with a file of evidence he
had against their suspect including the matching fingerprints. He arrived at Judge Bellingham's office at nine
fifteen. His secretary showed him right in.

"Judge, Bellingham, we really need a search
warrant for our suspect's house. Here is the evidence
we have on him so far including his matching fingerprints with those found at two of our five homicides.
We're afraid he might leave the country if we don't
move quickly."

Judge Bellingham was a short stiff man who took no
guff from anyone. He had gray hair neatly parted and
wore a proper suit and white shirt. He looked at the
folder and the fingerprints and nodded.

"Yes, the prints alone would be evidence enough for
me to issue a search warrant. What specifically are you
searching for?"

The Chief had been this route before. He listed a

number of thing including items of clothing or other items from the kill sites.

The judge made notes on a piece of paper. When Chief Sanderson was done, he called in his secretary and told her to write up a search warrant for these items including weapons. A few minutes later the woman came back in and the judge signed the warrant. He handed it to the Chief.

"Good luck. About time we caught this guy."

Chief Sanderson drove back to Forest Glen and called in all four of his officers. When they were in his office he laid it out.

"We have a search warrant for the address where Ed lives with his mother, the Rathwood Manor. I'd like to catch him there, but little chance of that. This is a no knock warrant, so we can go in if Mrs. Rathwood isn't there, or no one is there. Joanie will print out a list of items that we legally can search for and take away. It's a broad list and includes any items that any of the victims may have owned or worn, any newspaper clippings of the killings, anything that might tie Ed to the homicides. I expect no trouble other than some outrage from Elmira Rathwood. It will be good for her. Let's go."

Mrs. Rathwood was cooperative when Chief Sanderson told her what he was looking for.

"I'm sure you'll find nothing of the kind here," she said. "Chief, you should know we Rathwood's better than that."

"Yes, ma'am, but we must search anyway."

She led them to Ed's wing of the large home and showed them the six rooms. They went over the rooms carefully, found his clothes, his gun collection, including four fully automatic weapons that they confiscated

Elmira protested. "Edward told me that all of his guns were legal and some of them historic."

"Some are but the submachine guns are not."

She invited them to search her quarters, but the Chief declined. "We have no cause to suspect you of anything, Mrs. Rathwood," he told her.

"Well thank you for small favors."

Long and Hardy came back from the garage.

"We found four cars including a black Lexus that looks familiar, but we can't tie it to anything. Looks as if one car is missing."

"How many cars does the family have?" The Chief asked,

"Goodness, I'm not sure. I have just one, the new Cadillac Esplanade. I'm not sure how many Edward has."

"Chief, in back we found a locked door. Looks like it has two or three locks on it."

The Chief looked at Mrs. Rathwood. She shook her head.

"Oh, that door leads upstairs over the garage where some of the help used to stay when we had a live in maid. Now she comes from seven to seven, so she doesn't live up there."

"Do you have the keys? We need to check it out as well."

"I'm not sure. We put new locks on because one of our fired maids didn't return her key to the house or the apartment up there."

"That's all right," the Chief said. "We'll break off the locks. Our right if you want to read the warrant."

Mrs. Rathwood said nothing. She backed away and left them as they headed for the garage.

The Chief's car had a set of burglar tools, including a power drill, crowbar, nail puller, five pound sledge hammer and various screw driver and chisels. It took the men five minutes to rip the locks off the door and pry it open.

Hardy was first up the stairs and a moment later he bellowed in surprise.

"Get in here and look at this," he yelled. The police all went into the middle room that had been a bedroom. Now it was a display area. At once they saw the letterman's warm-up jacket that Willy had been wearing the afternoon he was picked up by the killer. They found the dress that Charlotte Alberts was wearing when she was kidnapped in the park.

"A collector," the Chief said. "We'll find something here from every one of the five killings. Olson, you have your camera in the car?"

"Yes sir."

"Go get it. I want you to take fifteen or twenty pictures in here detailing everything that we can see. We grab all of this evidence and take it with us. Then we'll dig into that set of drawers over there and see what else we can find. Damn but this is good. Now the DA will give us a warrant for Ed. Until we get it, I want him to be picked up as a person of interest. No arrest until we get the warrant, but if we find him, we nab him."

ED HAD LEFT his home early that morning with the plan of going fishing over on the Wilson River. He checked in at the store first. Uriah had come to work at seven o'clock to get some work done before the store opened. He had a few papers for Ed to sign and some questions about the new building.

Ed was tied up there until nearly ten o'clock. He was upset that he hadn't hit either of the cops with the Uzi last night. Now he would settle down, work his original plan for Hardy Jones in his new building. But first he needed some release at the river.

He still drove the Jeep that looked more like a military model than the sleek new car types. He had in it his police scanner and radio, and his fishing pole and tackle box. Under the front seat he had the Uzi and the historic colt wrapped in a towel. He looked at his fishing poles. He really needed another one, a fly rod that he liked to use sometimes. He headed for the house out at the edge of town.

He saw cars at the end of the drive at the Rathwood Manor and slowed to take a better look. Three police cars. He made no move to drive in, rather rolled by at a normal rate of speed, then took the next side street, and dove half a mile away back toward the center of town. He parked at the curb and thought it over.

The cops could be there looking for him. They could be there to find his DNA and his prints. If so they would find them. Or they might be there with a search warrant. In any case, his cover was blown. From now on he would be a wanted man. He would live out of his Jeep and after that he would pick up from a special file at work the new identity papers and bank accounts his mother had fashioned for his new life.

Should he leave now, get luggage in Portland, and stuff them with clothes off the rack? Then he could take the next flight to New York and then to France. Or should he do Officer Jones first?

He made his decision quickly. Jones had been a thorn in his gut for too long. He had to go. He'd use the scanner tonight if Jones was on duty and use the beer bust in one of the unfinished buildings at the new shopping center. If Jones was not on duty, he'd take him down at his house. That might mean killing the body guard cop and Jones' wife. Ed shrugged. Two more would be no problem for him. Until dark he had to be invisible. He couldn't go fishing because that's what he told Uriah that he was going to do. Surely the police would send a patrol car over to the Wilson River to check. No he had to take a drive into the hills. But first he'd stop and get a couple of chicken dinners at a drive though. No sense being hungry all day. He'd have a busy night one way or the other. Then he'd drive to Portland, about twenty five miles away, and stay in a motel with his new ID. In the morning he'd get one suitcase, a dragger with wheels, and buy enough clothes to last him for a week or so. Yes. It was good at last to have a firm date to get headed for France and those beautiful French girls.

41

IT WAS an afternoon meeting of all four of the Forest Glen Police Department officers in the Chief's office.

"Okay, troops. We have the warrant for the arrest of Edward Rathwood on a charge of five homicides. We grab him whenever we can. We'll put one man watching his furniture store, and one on his house out at Rathwood Manor."

"The store has two entrances," Olson said. "One in back off the alley."

"So we put two men on the store. Anything else?"

"He should be driving that military looking Jeep we saw out at the construction site," Hardy said. "His other cars are in the garage"

"What about his office at the store," Young asked. "He has a small office upstairs."

Chief Sanderson swore. "Damnit, I should have that address listed on the search warrant. We could go back and get another warrant."

"Probably too late," Hardy said. "If he saw us at his family mansion, he'll be wary might be running."

"Right," the Chief said. "I made a call to the Portland PD. They are putting his name on a watch list at every ticket seller's window at the airport. If he tries to buy a ticket, they nail him fast."

The Chief looked at his men. "Hardy, I want you on his house. Park down the street a ways in your own car. Young, you and Turley take his business—one in front, one in back. Olson, you're on patrol, cruising the town, watching for his Jeep. Let's move."

ED RATHWOOD KNEW he was a hunted man. He had called his mother an hour ago and she told him they had been to the house with a search warrant and raided his secret room over the garage.

"I'd think by now they have a warrant for your arrest. Drive to Portland now. Don't take any more chances."

"Just one more little task, Mother dear. Then I'll bug out of here and you won't have to worry about your criminal son anymore."

"I do worry. Be careful."

They hung up and Ed realized that he didn't have all of the money, his new identity papers, and charge cards. They were in that leather envelope his mother had put them in. He had taken it and put it in that secret compartment in his office desk. He had to get into the office. Ed knew there would be cops watching the front and back doors. He had to figure out how to get in without being seen.

He drove back to within two blocks of the office in the Jeep. Parked it legally, and took out a quart plastic jar of gasoline from the back seat. He walked past the end of the alley. There was no police car up there waiting. Two cars, but he recognized both that usually parked there. There were lots of places a cop could hide waiting and watching. He chose the car nearest the alley mouth and slipped up beside it. One window was half open. He poured the quart of gasoline into the passenger's side front set. He waited a moment, then struck a paper match and tossed it through the window.

The resulting whoosh of the exploding gasoline vapors wasn't loud enough to attract attention and Ed had jumped back to avoid it. He slipped out of the alley and waited. Moments later the car was burning furiously from the gasoline soaked seats. He saw two men rush out of the rear door of stores. One carried a fire extinguisher. Then he saw a uniformed cop leave a spot near the furniture store's back door and run down to the fire. He was using a cell phone as he ran.

A minute later there were a dozen people around the fire. The man with the fire extinguisher wasn't making any progress on putting out the flames. Ed walked up to the group, looked at the fire, then went on up the alley to his own back door and slipped inside. The last he saw of the cop, he was waving people back from the blazing car.

It took Ed only two minutes to get the foot square leather envelope with the zipper top. He slipped it inside his shirt, buttoned it, and went back down the stairs. Uriah was busy with a customer and didn't see him.

Ed went to the back door and looked out. No fire engine had responded yet. The cop was looking the other way. Ed went out the door into the alley and walked the opposite way away from the fire.

Five minutes later he was in his Jeep heading back into the farming country around town. A farm looking Jeep did not stand out in the country the way it did in town. He'd be safe out here until dark. Then he had two projects left.

BY FIVE O'CLOCK THAT AFTERNOON, the officers reported to the chief by radio or cell phone. No one had seen Ed or the Jeep. Bob Young reported the fire in the alley leading up to the furniture store's back entrance. The Chief groaned.

"So, Young, you left your post and went down to help with the fire?"

"Well, yeah, it seemed like the thing to do rather than just sit there."

"Ever heard of a diversion, Young? There's a chance that Ed needed something from his office and he set the damn car on fire to get you out of your watching place."

"Oh, damn. I saw the fire and I reacted."

"Were there lots of people around the fire?"

"Well, fires always attracts a crowd. Maybe ten or fifteen."

"And one of them could have been Ed walking right past you and up to the furniture store's back door."

"Goddamn. Sorry, Chief."

"Sorry doesn't help one hell of a lot. Anybody else run into anything unusual?" Nobody responded on the radio. "Okay. Everyone stay in place. I'm bringing burgers, shakes, and coffee for the four of you. Olson, meet me at the Better Burger in ten minutes."

. . .

IT WAS FULLY DARK when Ed drove his Jeep into the maze of small streets immediately behind the Manor house. Two of the streets led up to the family place that was completely hidden from this area. He paused at the end of the street and checked to see if there was any cop cars or other cars lurking around. He didn't think they would put a stake out person back here. They would have the front covered.

He didn't see any cars at all so he parked and walked up to the wooden rail fence that guarded the manor property.

Five minutes later, Ed paused at the edge of the woods and checked the house. He could see some lights on, but no police. He walked casually to the back door, used a key to unlock it, and slipped inside. He had realized today that his mother could be a threat to him. She could blow his cover in France and give his other name to police. He couldn't allow that.

He found her in the kitchen sipping at a glass of wine after a frozen dinner. She must have fired the cook again.

"Good evening, Mother."

She looked up, startled. "I didn't hear you come in. Didn't the police see you?"

"I came in the back way, Mother. You know they are out in front."

"They can't help you much, Mother." He took out a switch blade knife from his pocket. It was six inches long and honed to a razor edge.

"What in the world, Edward?"

"You know too much about me, Mother. I can't allow that."

He lunged forward and swiped the blade at her chest but she lifted her arms in automatic defense. The blade slashed across her forearm bringing a gout of blood, and a scream from Elmira.

"Edward, I would never..."

She didn't get it finished. He drew the blade back and stabbed her in the chest. He wasn't sure if he hit her heart or not, but Elmira Rathwood slumped against the kitchen table then crumpled to the floor.

She didn't move. He panted from the emotion of the moment, then calmed himself, and looked at his mother. She was turning pale. She didn't move.

"Good bye, Mother," he said and slipped out of the kitchen just as the other kitchen door opened and Bonita, the new maid, rushed in and screamed. His door closed before she saw him.

Edward retraced his steps out of the house and through the woods to his Jeep. Now, he had tied up another loose end. Only one more to go. Hardy Jones. In his Jeep he turned on the receiver to the local police channel and waited for some activity. It was a quiet night.

Officer Olson was sent to a small accident on Tenth Street. He wondered how long the cops would stay on their stakeouts. That would foil his try at a beer bust call to get Hardy to the King Shopping Center. If Jones was in a police car, he would use the radio to report in. Until that time, Ed had to wait. He thought about his mother. He had hated her ever since she had made him watch her kill that dog out at the lake. Now the hatred washed away. She was dead and so was his hatred.

He settled down to wait with some cool jazz on the

Jeep radio just loud enough he could hear but so it wouldn't mess up the next police radio call. He had to wait, so did Officer Jones.

42

OFFICER HARDY JONES came alert as a siren split the Oregon night air and an ambulance raced past him and careened around the corner into the Rathwood Manor driveway. Hardy started his car and followed it in.

A young Mexican girl stood at the big double doors and waved at the ambulance. Hardy parked near it and ran up to the driver who just got out of the rig.

"Lady hurt here," the Mexican girl said.

Two more para-medics opened the rear door and the first man hurried inside behind the girl. Hardy followed. They went to the kitchen.

Hardy smelled the blood as soon as the door opened.

"*Muerto?*" the girl asked.

The medic touched the throat of the woman on the floor and shook his head. "She's still alive, but just barely. Lost a lot of blood."

The other two medics came in with a gurney. They lowered it to the floor, then the three men transferred her gently to the platform. One of them started to take her blood pressure.

"No time, we can do that in the rig. Let's get her out there and start an IV. Gonna be touch and go."

"Hillsboro?" Hardy asked.

"Closest one," the driver said and they wheeled Mrs. Rathwood out of the kitchen. Hardy motioned to the girl.

"You see who did this?"

She shook her head. "No see. Door over there closing when I come in. Hear missus scream."

"But you saw nobody?"

"No see."

Hardy opened the door the girl had pointed to. It led to a store room, then a utility room and an outside door. The door to the back yard was unlocked. Beyond all he could see was the edge of a swimming pool, a tennis court, and then the dark shadows of a large growth of Douglas fir trees and brush. He knew that past the trees were three or four streets filled with modest houses. He retraced his steps and found the Mexican girl cleaning up the blood from the kitchen floor.

He took her name, gave her his card, and said he might need to talk to her again. In his car, Hardy called the station on his cell. The Chief came on at once.

"Knifing out here at the Rathwood Manor. Mrs. Rathwood is on her way to the hospital barely alive. She was slashed and stabbed. The Mexican maid interrupted the attack. She didn't see the person, but evidently scared him off before he could finish the job."

"Any suspects?"

"Could be Ed. His mother must have known about

the secret room and the trophies there. Maybe he is running and wanted to shut up a deadly witness against him,"

"Yeah, could be. Where's Fred?"

"Came down with the flu. Cindy is nursing him back to a no vomit basis."

"So you be careful. You say he didn't come in the front way, so he must have come through the woods in back."

"Probably."

"You stay on watch there. He might not have had time to get what he went to get from the house. Or he just might have gone there to kill his mother. This guy has got to go down."

Hardy stayed at his post half a block down from the entrance to the Rathwood Manor driveway. He didn't think that Ed would try the house again, even if he didn't get what he needed. Hardy nodded off once, sat ramrod straight, and opened both windows. He wished he had some more coffee.

By twelve thirty, Chief Sanderson called him and told him to pack it in and go home. Hardy didn't argue.

ED SAT AND WAITED, listening to the local police radio. It was a quiet night, again. It took him an hour to realize that only Olson was on the radio. He had answered another accident and a lost dog call. That meant Hardy Jones was in his private car without a radio and communicating with his cell phone.

Ed swore for five minutes, using up every appropriate word he could think of and then started repeating himself. He started the Jeep and drove toward Hardy's house. Hardy had to go down for sure and the other two if they recognized him or got in the way. Hell, one, two, or three, it made no difference. But Hardy was the important one.

THREE HOUSES from Hardy's place Ed saw a for sale sign in the front yard of a house. It had a side drive. He parked and went up and looked in the front window. No furniture. Nobody home. He hurried back to his Jeep and backed it up the side drive until it was hidden beside the house. He was across the street and two houses down from Officer Hardy Jones' place. Perfect. Hardy's Ford was not in the drive in front of the garage where he usually parked.

Ed walked down one house, went across the street, and slid in beside some evergreen shrubs next to the front of the house next door to Hardy's. He was about fifty feet from the driveway. No closer hiding spot. He'd play it as it fell.

Ed waited. He realized that he was good at waiting. He'd been doing enough of it lately. His watch showed that it was twelve thirty. He hoped that Hardy wasn't on an overnight stay at his stakeout.

Ed leaned back against the house. He came awake in a rush. A car had driven past. He looked at the glowing numbers on his watch. Just after one A.M. He must have slept for half an hour. No more. He did hand exercises, then began adding numbers starting with two. Two and two were four. Four and four were eight, eight and eight were sixteen. Sixteen and sixteen were thirty two.

By the time he was up into the thousands he gave

up. He had never been that good at math. Where the hell was Hardy Jones? As he thought it, a car came around the corner half a block down, slowed and turned into Hardy Jones' drive. Jones hurried out and ran up the side walk, used a key, and was inside before Ed could get his legs uncurled and working right,

Now to plan B. He slipped out of the shrubs and walked around to the back of the Jones house. The back door was on a patio, but it was a wooden door not a sliding glass one. The house was fifty years old and the lock was rudimentary. Ed pulled a screw driver from his pocket with a quarter inch blade on the end.

He found the door handle and pushed the screw driver's flat side into the area between the door and the door jamb. Right in there was a bolt that slid into that lock. The bolt had a slanted surface and with enough pressure, the bolt would pop back and unlock the door. He forced the screw driver in twice then took off his shoe and when he thought he was in the right spot, he pounded sharply on the end of the screwdriver handle. It slid inward and the door lock opened. He held the door knob in his hand and waited without moving or making a sound for two minutes. Nothing sounded inside the house. No one came to investigate. He pushed the door open silently and waited again. No reaction from inside.

Ed didn't know the floor plan of the house and that was a worry. Probably two bedrooms. Would the guard dog man sleep on the couch? Probably. There was one night light glowing in the room just ahead. The kitchen. Beyond that he saw another faint glow. He moved there silently. It was a living room and had a couch on the far side. He held his Colt revolver in his right hand and the

Uzi on a cord around his neck. He couldn't see if anyone was on the couch against the far wall. The voice came as a shock and he lifted the Colt.

"One more step and you're a dead man," the voice roared.

Ed fired a round at the sound of the voice. Too late he realized his mistake. This was a silent mission. A shot came back at him, hit him in the shoulder, and spun him around. A form lifted up from the couch and Ed fired again, hitting the man in the chest and slamming him backward.

Ed charged forward, forgetting the pain in his shoulder. He found the gun the man had used. Ed grabbed it and started to run down the hall. To his surprise a shot blasted in front of him, but it missed. Ed crouched but could see nothing in the blackness. If he fired, he'd give away his position. He was against a door on the right. He reached for the knob and turned it slowly. Unlocked. He pushed it open and surged inside, slamming it shut. He found the room light switch and pushed it. The light flooding the room blinded him for a moment then he saw it was a bedroom. A woman sat up on the bed, long blonde hair falling around her shoulders.

"Well now, you must be Cindy. I've heard a lot about you."

Hardy lay flat on the hall floor and punched up the Chief's cell phone number on his auto dialer and waited two rings.

"Yes, so?"

"Chief. Hardy. Ed is in my house and he has captured Cindy. I think he shot Fred. I could use some help."

43

HARDY JONES BEAT down the panic that engulfed him. Ed was in the spare bedroom where Cindy had been sleeping some nights. He couldn't have known she was there. Now what the hell did he do? There would be no backup help arriving for ten or fifteen minutes and even then what could they do? Maybe he could talk the man out? Fat chance. He held all the cards and he must know it. Hardy got to his feet and moved toward the spare bedroom door. What could he do? A shadow near the end of the hall startled Hardy.

"It's me," Fred whispered. "I'm shot but not down. He got my Glock. Cindy in there?"

Hardy nodded in the dim light coming from the night light in the hall. "Fred, what can we do?"

Fred slid past the bedroom door until he was next to Hardy then he whispered. "He's got the advantage. He wants you not her so we don't do anything heroic or stupid. He'll try to use Cindy for bait so he can gun you down. I should send you driving away from here."

"I won't do that."

"Didn't think so. Okay. Go past the door, out the front door, and over to the bedroom window. He probably has the lights on. See if you can spot him in the bedroom. I'll cause a ruckus out here to distract him. If you can get a clean shot at him, blast away. He should come to the door. Can you see the door from that window?"

"Yes. If I have a shot I'll shoot right through the glass."

"Right, so go."

Hardy went past the bedroom door without a sound and to the front door. He went out and around to the bedroom window. The lights were on and the drape had not been pulled. He edged up to look into the room. He had his Glock ready to fire. At first he didn't see Ed, then he edged up more and he could see him standing against the wall next to the door. But he was holding Cindy in front of him. No chance for a shot. Hardy heard the pounding that Fred must be doing on the bedroom door. He heard Ed laugh and his words came softly.

"No way, asshole. I've got all the chips here. Get Hardy out in the hall where I can see him. Then Cindy and I will come out."

Hardy felt the sweat dripping off his nose. He had to do something. He used the muzzle of the Glock to break the bedroom window. That caused Ed to jump in surprise and half turn toward the window. By then Hardy had sighted in on the killer and fired one shot at his head which extended a foot over Cindy's short frame. The round missed and Ed lifted the Glock and fired four times through the window and into the window sill. Hardy and dropped to the ground as soon as he saw he had missed. He wiped sweat from his eyes. What now? He could try another shot, but Ed would be watching for him to lift up. He wondered what Fred was doing. The pounding on the door had stopped.

He looked up at the window and saw the muzzle of a Glock come out and fire three times downward. Hardy had just time enough to dive away from the window before the shots came. Then he heard a crash from inside the bedroom. He had no idea what it was.

Fred had used his experience with barricaded doors to help the situation. He stood back at the side of the hall and charged forward, kicking out with his right boot with all the force of his two hundred pounds behind it. The old push and turn lock sprang open and the door slammed inward. Fred lunged away from the open door, hit the floor, and rolled against the wall away from the open door.

"Give it up Rathwood," Fred said. "You're surrounded. All you can hope for are about six non-fatal gunshot wounds."

"Not a chance. I've captured your queen. You can't win without her. I'll trade you even up. One live queen for one shot dead Hardy Jones."

"You're dreaming, Ed. Not a chance. You harm one blonde hair on her head and you're dead meat. I've dealt with assholes like you before."

"Big talker, Fred. Sure I know who you are." Ed fired two rounds through the open door chest high. They plowed into the painted wall on the other side of the hall.

Fred edged close to the open door at the carpet level, then jolted his head out, looked at the room, and jerked back. Ed had Cindy in front of him using her as a shield. Not enough of Ed showed to let Fred take a shot with his hideout .38. Fred heard sirens in the distance. What good would they do? It was a standoff. Anybody made a move and he or she got killed.

Hardy heard the sirens. He ran away from the house down fifty yards in the direction he thought the Chief or squad cars would come. He was right. The Chief's car rolled up and stopped where Hardy waved. He rolled down the window.

"Chief, he's got Cindy in the first bedroom. I got a shot through the window but missed. When he turned I saw an Uzi hanging from a cord around his neck. What can we do?"

"How is Fred?"

"Shot in the shoulder or somewhere, but he's walking and talking. He's in the hall. Only thing I can think of is tear gas, try to drive him outside."

"Does the window you broke open?"

"Yes, all the way, it's a crank out. The screen came off and I never replaced it."

"Tear gas sounds like our only option."

Hardy's cell phone rang. He grabbed it. "Fred?"

"Right. He's still inside, holding Cindy as a shield. I kicked in the door, but no chance for a shot. I saw that he has an Uzi."

"Roger that. We're thinking about tear gas. Can you get out of there?"

"Rather guard the hall, so he can't come this way. I've tasted tear gas before. Fire away."

The Chief parked the car and opened the trunk. He took out four tear gas grenades.

"These are new. They go off on contact so no chance to throw them back,"

"Used them before," Hardy said. "Pull the pin and throw. I'll get just below the window so I can't miss. How will Cindy take this?"

"It may give her a chance to get away and run down the hall. We'll just have to wait and see."

Hardy took two of the grenades and ran back to his house, slid along the front wall to the bedroom, and knelt beside the broken window. He pulled the pin and tossed a grenade into the room. As soon as it hit he heard a hissing sound and then the scream from Cindy. He knew it was her.

Inside the bedroom, Cindy screamed again, then began fighting him. She kicked his shins with backward blows with her heels. She got one hand free and clawed at his face. He slapped her. She caught his hand and bit one finger until it bled. He hit her again then they both began to cough

Cindy tried to rub her eyes, but couldn't reach them. She squirmed around until she faced him. He still had his arm around her shoulders. She pushed and charged ahead. He was taken by surprise and backed up, stumbled over the end of the bed, and let loose of her to catch himself.

Cindy ran for the door. She heard the gunfire behind her but didn't feel anything as she ran through the door into the hall. Fred caught her and ran with her into the living room and then pushed her out the front door. He went back to patrol the hall.

Twice Ed tried to get into the hall. Twice Fred drove him back with a pair of shots at him that missed.

Hardy threw the second tear gas grenade into the room and stood back from the window. Bob Young jumped out of his patrol car on the other side of

Hardy's house. He advanced cautiously using his cell phone for instructions.

In a surprise move, Ed Rathwood kicked out the rest of the roll out window and jumped to the ground three feet away. He hit on his feet and saw Hardy lifting his Glock. He snapped off two shots from his Glock, then sprinted around the house away from Hardy. All three of the policemen fired at Ed as he rounded the house and they charged after him.

44

HARDY HAD PULLED BACK from the window after he threw in the second tear gas grenade to avoid the gas blowing out. When he saw the window kicked out he moved back a step and was surprise when Ed leaped out and raced around the corner of the house into the back yard. There was no fence in front.

Hardy was first in the chase with the other police farther away. He sprinted around the house and paused. Ahead he saw a figure at the far side fence lift a weapon. A moment later the Uzi stuttered out a half dozen rounds and Hardy hit the dirt just before the lead slugs pounded through the air around him. Hardy got off two shots, but he was fifty feet away and wasn't sure if he hit Ed. The killer grabbed the top of the six foot wooden fence, lifted up and rolled over it before Hardy could get off another shot.

"He went over the fence next door to the left," Hardy bellowed. The Chief and Young evidently didn't hear him. They ran around the side of the house with weapons up.

"He went into the yard next door," Hardy said. "He may be trying for the street."

"I'll go over the fence," Young said and charged it, grabbed the top, and went over in one smooth move.

By the time Hardy and the Chief got around Hardy's house and to the sidewalk, they could find no one running. Nobody was on the street. They moved cautiously into the yard next door then on toward the second house. They had just touched the lawn of the second house when a blast of Uzi rounds made them dive for the grass. The rounds were aimed to their left and neither man was hit. Young came out of the yard of the first house just in time to see a vehicle blast down the driveway beside the house. It had been hidden.

"That's his Jeep," Hardy brayed and all three fired at the rig as it jolted into the street and turned to the right. All three men ran for their cars. Hardy was in the street after the Jeep first and realized that the getaway Jeep did not have its lights on. The only time Hardy saw it was when it went under a street light. Hardy sensed that the rig was heading for the countryside, not down town. Out there he would need his lights to stay on the narrow roads. Hardy used his cell phone to let the other two know where Ed seemed to be heading.

The Chief and Young talked on the police radio. Hardy lost the Jeep at the edge of town. It was heading south out toward Gaston. Lots of country roads out there but all unlighted. Hardy slowed, then saw lights come on a quarter of a mile ahead, and the red tail lights marked the route. He raced ahead, taking the turns as fast as he dared and hitting high speeds on the straight-aways. The car could outrun the Jeep in any kind of road. Now Hardy pulled closer and closer to the Jeep until he was less than fifty yards away. The road straightened out past a dairy and small farms. Hardy punched the accelerator and closed the gap.

For his trouble he got a blast of Uzi rounds from the Jeep as Ed fired out the window with one hand. One round hit the passenger's side of the windshield and put a hundred cracks in the glass. Then the Jeep started around a sudden turn but was going too fast and slewed sideways. It jolted into a shallow ditch and rolled over. Hardy pulled up behind the wreck wondering if Ed had survived the crash. He got out of his car but kept it between himself and the wreck. A moment later the Uzi spoke again with a twelve round burst. Most of the rounds hit the car. Hardy had ducked behind the rear of the car when he heard the report. He wasn't hit. So, Ed had survived and still had teeth. The other two police cars raced up and stopped behind Hardy's vehicle. The lawmen both left their rigs and joined Hardy behind his car.

"He's alive and shooting the Uzi," Hardy said. "He might try for the woods over there. There's a farm house a half mile down that still has lights on."

"Let me try to outflank him," Young said. "I'll go up the road a hundred yards, into that pasture across the fence, and wait and see if he comes that way."

"Go," the Chief said.

"I'll get him on this side," Hardy said. "Don't try to rush him, Chief. He's still got lots of rounds in that Uzi." Hardy ran silently down the road twenty yards, slipped through the shallow ditch, and between the top two strands of the barbed wire fence. He moved ten yards toward the crash, lay down in the short grass of the pasture, and waited and listened.

At first he heard nothing but a few crickets chirping away. Then he sensed more than heard a low moaning sound. It increased and then faded. Could Ed be injured in the wreck? In the faint moonlight he could see the Jeep where it lay on its side. He couldn't see it well enough to know if Ed was still inside or on the ground. Ed wasn't the type to wear a seat belt.

Five minutes later Young called Hardy's cell phone. He caught it on the first buzz then rolled six feet to the left in case Ed heard it.

"Yes," he whispered.

A whisper came back. "Thought I saw some movement inside the Jeep but not certain. I think he's hurt."

"I heard what I thought was a groan."

"Yeah, me too. I'm going to put four rounds into the wreck. Stay low." The four shots blasted in the quiet, cool Oregon countryside. The sound echoed off into the distance. There was no reaction from the wreck. Was he hit, dead, or playing possum? Hardy couldn't tell. Then the submachine gun chattered again. Six rounds this time aimed back at Young's position. Instantly Hardy tried to count rounds. How many in an Uzi magazine? Twenty, thirty? He didn't know. He had heard at least twenty five rounds fired. Maybe the magazine was dry. Hardy's cell phone buzzed. He whispered a hello. It was the Chief.

"I think he's hurt. He's still well armed. We fire at will. Empty your magazines and put in new ones. Let's end this."

Moments later all three men opened fire at the crashed Jeep. The rounds came from both sides and the road. They each fired about twenty rounds then stopped.

"Thought I heard a scream," Young reported when the firing ceased. "I'll go in and check. Hey, I had my army training."

"Be careful and have a full magazine," the Chief said.

They waited. Hardy edged forward another five yards.

They waited.

Then Young shouted. "All clear. We've got a dead body up here. Move in."

They all trained their flashlights on the wreck. Ed Rathwood's crumpled body lay on the driver's door. His feet had been pinned against the firewall when the engine crashed through. He had more than a dozen bullet wounds in his chest and head.

The Chief gave a long sigh. "I'm glad this is over. I'll call the Sheriff so he can get his team out here first thing in the morning. Hardy. I want you to stand guard here until the County Mounties arrive. I called the station. They sent an ambulance out to your house and took Fred to the hospital. Cindy is waiting at the station. Give them a call to let her know you're all right. Medics said Fred took that round high in his chest, over his lung and missed his clavicle. An in and out, they said."

Hardy nodded in the glare of the flashlights. "Not like we didn't give Ed a chance. He had plenty of chances to surrender."

"Don't worry about it, Hardy. You did good. Now we'll let the county take over. We're well out of the city limits."

45

BY NOON THE NEXT DAY, order had pretty well returned to the Forest Glen Police department station. The sheriff had taken over the accident and shootout at the dangerous corner well south of town. All three police at the site had been questioned. Cindy had been questioned by the sheriff's detectives as well and they would talk to Fred later in the day at the Hillsboro hospital.

In a big city police department, shooters in a fatality would be put on desk jobs and not returned to the field until after an investigation. Forest Glen didn't have that many cops so the Sheriff had notes put in their official duty jackets and they returned to work.

Chief Sanderson drove to Hillsboro to talk with Mrs. Rathwood. She was out of danger now, despite some serious internal bleeding. Repair work had been done and she was recovering nicely. The sheriff had told her about the death of her son. The Chief found her talking with her lawyer.

When her lawyer had left, the Chief went in and asked her a question that had bothered him.

"Mrs. Rathwood, do you know who attacked you in your own home?"

"Yes, it was my son Edward. He was out of his mind yelling and screaming. If my maid hadn't come rushing in when I screamed, he would have killed me. She saved my life."

"Why would he do you any harm?"

"He was out of his mind, like I said. Half crazy for some weird reason. He was trying to rob me and run away to Paris. He had papers all set to give him a new identity. Did you find any papers like that in his vehicle?"

"The sheriff didn't say that they found anything like that. I'm sure he would have told me if they did."

"Chief Sanderson. I am truly sorry for the tragedies that Edward caused in our town. It's probably my fault. I should have seen the signs long before he went completely mad. I feel a great love for our little town, and I am going to make some restitution. I know I can't bring back the lives that he ended. But I can do something to make life a little easier for the city, the college, and the families who lost members."

"I've instructed my lawyer to send checks to the five families in the amount of five hundred thousand dollars for each one. I know money can't replace a loved one but it may help in the long run. To the city I am going to send a grant of five million dollars to be used for schools, the fire department, and the police department. Again, I know that money does not wipe out a hatred for my family and our name. However I hope it will make that hatred a little less hurtful."

Chief Sanderson stared at her with a growing understanding. Her son had harmed the town more than he could ever realize. Now his mother was trying to compensate some way for his crimes.

"Mrs. Rathwood. I really don't know what to say. I'm sure the City Council, the families, and the college will appreciate your generosity.

Now if you will give me an account of how you were attacked, I'll put it in my file and close this case."

She did.

She smiled when he left. It was a good thing that she had kept duplicate copies of all the papers and bank books she had worked up for Edward. If some of them were found it wouldn't matter since she had told the police about them. She had just told her lawyer to visit her home and bring back to her the two bank account emails from the two Swiss banks. She had written the accounts with dual signers. So either she or Edward could make withdrawals. In the next few days she would take all of the money out of both accounts and return the four million to her industrial account in one of her Portland banks. The other small matter she would take care of in person once out of the hospital. She would sell the Rathwood Fine Furniture store and the projected new store, its stock and goodwill for one dollar to Uriah Condit. He deserved it. Yes, that would be good.

She stared at the clinical white walls of her hospital room. Edward, oh Edward my son. How could you have gone so far astray? I was only playing with you with that dog I killed. I really didn't kill that maid. She stole a thousand dollars from me and rushed down to Mexico.

Edward, did I teach you and push you into being a psychopathic killer?

CHIEF SANDERSON SAT at his desk in the station. Fred would be out of the hospital in a week. The Chief had planned to hire him full time. He also had laid out what he wanted when the check for five million hit the city coffers. There would be three new patrolmen, a sergeant's pay for Hardy Jones, three new squad cars, and a new communications system with computers in each police car for instant reports and instructions.

HARDY JONES SAT at his desk flipping paper clips into a coffee cup. The chief had told them about the five million the city would get from Mrs. Rathwood but swore them to secrecy until she announced it herself and turned over the check.

He thought about the final shootout with Ed. IT bothered him but the Sheriff said there would be no ballistic checking, so no one would know which one of the three Glock pistols fired the bullet that killed Ed Rathwood. He wouldn't dwell on it. It could have been him. It could have been one of the other two. He put it out of his mind. He would not let it bother him anymore.

Cindy had come through the kidnapping and tear gas without any harmful effects. She could even joke about it now and then. She did seem different. Yesterday she didn't want to eat any breakfast. This morning she tried to eat some oatmeal but hurried from the table. He heard her retching in the bathroom. He frowned. Why was she sick in the morning? Then it hit him—morning sickness? Could it be? He grabbed his cell phone and hit the home speed dial button.

Could it be? Could it be?

IF YOU LIKED THIS, YOU MIGHT LIKE:

GATEWAYS TO ANNIHILATION: STORIES
BY JARRET KEENE

"Keene's collection is quietly magnificent. I can think of few things better than spending your time reading his words." – Mercedes M. Yardley, two-time Bram Stoker Award-Winner

A cursed pizzeria. A haunted B-movie legacy. A tycoon's final robotic companion.

Welcome to Gateways to Annihilation—a searing collection of horror short stories that seamlessly fuses right-here-and-right-now themes of war trauma, pandemic stress, religious terrorism, political extremism, cryptozoological mania, and the human hunger for a sudden cleansing apocalypse, while encouraging readers to reach for a bag of movie popcorn in the darkness of the night.

Author Jarret Keene conjures 14 twisted tales where monsters lurk in neon shadows and infernal items hold lives hostage. Whether it's a Japanese war vet trapped inside Hollywood rubber suits, a Vegas comic shop owner stalked by satanic forces, or a billionaire's android nurse with sinister protocols, each story spirals into the uncanny with razor precision. In this collection that melds the nostalgic eeriness of The Twilight Zone with the nihilistic bite of Black Mirror, victims and perpetrators dance in blood-spattered loops of fate. Perfect for fans of weird fiction and supernatural thrillers, Gateways to Annihilation is literary horror with a cult heart.

AVAILABLE NOW